PRAISE FOR *STORIES FROM THE CITY OF GOD*

"The essays or 'chronicles' in this collection are slight but marvelous...powerful...moving...In Marina Harss's lively translation, these 'chronicles' are more concrete and colorful than the furious polemics of Pasolini's last years...to which they make an excellent prelude." —*The Nation*

"What's ugly and squalid shows its beauty to Pasolini...The short pieces succeed as portraits of people and place during a certain time...The author opens up a window on hidden Rome, a part of the city that continues to exist in certain dodgy corners and presumably always will." —*Bloomsbury Review*

"The pieces in this collection suggest watercolor portraits of Rome and Romans as they were when Pasolini first moved to the city in 1949...a gorgeous account of Pasolini's itinerary, migrating between zones of cultural privilege and 'the lower depths.'...[T]hese occasional writings—some outtakes from his novels, others written for newspapers and journals—are suffused with an ecstatic love for the wiles and mannerisms, urban patois, and unconscious grace of the underclass. Pasolini's lightness of touch and breadth of observation combine in a gestural prose with a revolutionary purpose." —*Film Comment*

STORIES FROM THE CITY OF GOD
Sketches and Chronicles of Rome, 1950–1966

Pier Paolo Pasolini

Walter Siti, editor
Marina Harss, translator

Other Press • New York

Softcover edition 2019
ISBN 978-1-59051-997-4

A paperback edition of this book was published in Italian under the title
Storie della città di Dio; Racconti e cronache romane (1950–1966).

Copyright © Giulio Einaudi Editore, 1995

Translation copyright © 2003 Marina Harss

Production Editor: Robert D. Hack

This book was set in 11 pt. Celeste Regular by Alpha Graphics of Pittsfield, NH.

10 9 8 7 6 5 4 3 2 1

Library of Congress Cataloging-in-Publication Data

Pasolini, Pier Paolo, 1922–1975.
  [Storie della città di Dio. English]
  Stories from the city of God : sketches and chronicles of Rome, 1950–1966 /
Pier Paolo Pasolini ; translated by Marina Harss.
      p. cm.
  ISBN 1-59051-048-8
    I. Harss, Marina.   II. Title.

PQ4835.A48S7613 2003
853'.914—dc21

                                        2003040462

CONTENTS

TRANSLATOR'S NOTE

"In the winter of 1949, I fled with my mother to Rome, as in a novel." This is how Pier Paolo Pasolini later described, with his characteristic sense of drama, his move to Rome at the age of twenty-seven. With his escape from northern Italy, his Roman adventure began. A sexual scandal had destroyed his Friulian idyll, the first of a long series that would plague his life. He had spent his entire youth in the northern countryside, shielded to a great degree from the violence and repression of the Fascist regime, the war, and the subsequent destruction and poverty Italy experienced in this period. Yet once in Rome, he found himself poor and alone save for his beloved mother, in a city ravaged by war and then undergoing a period of intense change. He found his new home among the underprivileged, peripheral, marginalized classes who lived in the new projects built on the outskirts of the city, and in its ancient, rough, lower-class neighborhoods. He was witness to the beginning of a process that would transfigure the city into a modern, gentrified capital, a process that he feared and loathed and that finally drove him away. In his interview with Luigi Sommaruga that is included in this volume, Pasolini expresses his break with Rome in terms reminiscent of the end of a love affair: "It has changed, and I don't want to understand it any more."

In this volume, we detect an emotional cycle that begins with the shock of freedom and love that Pasolini felt when he first arrived in Rome and concludes with the disgust, sadness, and alienation that he felt toward the end of his life. At his first encounter with the city, he was deeply moved and fascinated by the contrasts and layers that were, and to a degree still are, its most defining feature. In "Roguish Rome," he writes, "Its beauty is a natural mystery. We can attribute it to the stratification of styles which at every angle offers up a new, surprising cross section; the excessive beauty produced by this superposition of styles is a veritable shock to the system. But would Rome be the most beautiful city in the world if it were not, at the same time, the ugliest?" When he speaks of beauty and ugliness, he is not simply evaluating architectural styles. What matters to Pasolini, the only thing that truly matters, are the people living in its various neighborhoods, slums, projects, and shantytowns. The beauty is to be found in the Roman *ragazzo* as well as in the sweep of the Tiber, and the ugliness lies in the torpor of the slums and the squalid lives of the people who live in them, and even more in the greed, oppression, and American-style commercialism that he sees taking over his beloved city and the whole country. For him, the greatest ugliness of all lies in the hypocrisy of power in all its forms, domestic and political. Thus a sense of place defines and completely infuses the mentality and attitudes of the people whose lives he witnesses, and both tentatively and passionately participates in.

Pasolini's vision of the city, then, is his portrait of its poor and marginalized, among whom he lived. They are people like Morbidone in "The Passion of the Lupin-Seller," or the young man selling chestnuts by the Trastevere bridge in "Trastevere Boy," and the boy who steals fish from the market in "The Dogfish." At first, the author is drawn to these characters by need, as he admits in "The Periphery of My Mind." "It was need, my own poverty, even if it was that of an unemployed member of the *bourgeoisie*, that drove me to the immediate human, vital experience of the world which I later described and continue to describe. I did not make a conscious choice, but rather it was a kind of compulsion of destiny." Beyond this, Pasolini feels an enormous admiration for their ability to prevail against the onslaught of "modern" *bourgeois* culture that pushes them further and further toward the fringes. This affection, even love, tinged with erotic attraction, fascinates him with the inner working of the minds of his characters as if they held the key to a sublime understanding. He writes of the chestnut-seller in "Trastevere Boy," "For my part, I would like to understand the mechanisms of his heart by which the Trastevere—shapeless, pounding, idle—lives inside of him. Where does the Tiber end and the boy begin?"

His answer is language, and in particular, dialect and slang. Pasolini's discovery of dialect marked a crucial moment in his youth, an awakening. This awakening occurred during the war, when he was nineteen and living in his mother's rural home town of Casarsa in Friuli. "I learned Friulian as a sort of mystical act of love," he said later in a 1969 interview. It became an almost religious, self-defining impulse to learn the local dialect and render a version of it in his writing. Through language, he deciphered a mysterious connection to the closed, pre-Christian world of the Friulian peasants, their relationship to nature and the outside world, and eventually, through an erotic relationship with a local boy, to his own sexuality. This experience of discovery would be repeated and expanded with the Roman underclass. In Casarsa, he began writing poetry and narrative sketches in Friulian dialect. At the time, his use of dialect was also a political statement; he was writing in a "lower form" of Italian at a time when the classical, heroic origins of Italian culture were being championed by the Fascist regime, which tried to suppress the identities of all subcultures and differences for the sake of national unity and the consolidation and centralization of power. For personal, esthetic, and political reasons, Pasolini instinctively placed himself on the outside, with the people he loved and their anomalous landscape and way of life. He was, at the same time, extremely self-conscious about his relationship to his chosen subjects and the use of their language. This operation of transcription of dialect was a conscious act and a political one, one that he knew might appear forced and artificial to his critics. His novels, *The Ragazzi* and *A Violent Life*, were, in fact, criticized by the Left for their ambiguous attitude toward their subjects and the manner in which he depicted the lives of the impoverished classes. One critic wrote of *The Ragazzi*, "Pasolini apparently depicts the world of the Roman sub-proletariat, but the real focus of his interest is his morbid taste for the dirty, abject, discomposed, and turbid." Pasolini defends himself in the Sommaruga interview, saying that "because each person must write what he knows, I had to become the witness of the Roman *borgata*. Biographical need was combined with the particular tendency of my eros. Therefore, even after the sociological need is satisfied, I continue to live by necessity on the periphery." He is linked to his subjects by his own marginalization, principally the result of his sexual desire.

Similarly, Pasolini learned the secrets of Rome through the language of its poorest inhabitants. With the help of Sergio Citti, a young hustler he met on one of his slum-crawls, and other "informants," he picked up their manner of speaking, their turns of phrase, and their rhetorical flourishes. To his mind, these linguistic forms revealed the reality of Rome, its psychology and cultural landscape. He described this highly self-conscious process in "The Periphery of My Mind," "If someone were to follow me in my daily life, they would often find me in a pizzeria in Torpignattara or the *borgata* of Alessandrina, Torre Maura, or Pietralata, writing down expressions, exclamations, and words taken directly from the mouth of 'speakers' who I have invited to speak for this very purpose." He transcribed phrases and verbal exchanges into his stories, and he devoted several essays to the relationship between these linguistic systems and the speakers' landscape. He felt that only through such language could he approach their raw, direct and untranslated experience.

How, then, does the translator deal with dialect and street slang? This is the first problem the translator encounters in these pieces, and it remains a principal concern throughout. All of the narrative sketches included in this volume contain examples of Roman slang, and many of the chronicles— mainly articles and essays—comment on the use of dialect. One of them, "Roman Slang," is an analysis of several words and rhetorical forms typical of Roman lowlifes. Dialect is a difficult challenge to any translator, as one of many for those who would render Pasolini's relentless, vibrant, poetic, and desperate style in English. There is nothing more alive than slang—it is the very heart of these texts, pumping life and immediacy into them. In it one hears the voice of the people of Pasolini's Rome, and without it, the sketches wither. However, there is nothing more difficult to keep alive than slang once it has been transplanted into a new text. Constant interventions must be undertaken to preserve the vitality of the original, organic text, which can resist a new language like a body rejects a new heart. American English has its own slang, or rather slangs. They are utterly untranslatable, even from one region or social group to another, and lose all meaning once they cross the Atlantic. So it is easy to imagine that Pasolini's slang, which is from a time, place, and social world far removed from its current translator and reader, would be doubly opaque. These very challenges of its translation draw it close to the experience of translating a kind of hermetic poetry. The process of rendering this dialect into another tongue, then, is a process of recuperation, of research, of historical and cultural curiosity, and of love perhaps, for language, Pasolini's language, and the language of Pasolini's subjects. Through this process the author and his translator create their own capacity to render humor, imagery, class, place, and humanity.

In translating these pieces, I have employed several approaches, each of them imperfect, each tailored to a specific situation. In the case of typical Roman exclamations, for example, I have often chosen to leave the words in the original dialect, supplying an explanation in a note. On one level, exclamations are the same in every language. They are meant to call attention to themselves, to punctuate the conversation, to surprise, to call out to another person. They are in some ways intelligible to the reader, even if he or she does not know exactly what the words mean. At least, such is my hope. Of course, their effect is enriched by the knowledge of what the words mean and also by their context. For example, Roman slang employs words associated with death much more than, say, Northern Italian slang, which tends more toward blasphemy and sexual imagery. "*Ammazzalo!*" is a typical Roman exclamation of surprise or awe. It means, literally "Kill it!" "*Li mortacci vostra*" is an insult against a person's dead relatives, but is used quite casually to tell someone to go to hell, and, in its more familiar form, "*li mortacci tua*," to greet a close friend one has not seen in a while. It expresses surprise, pleasure, and consternation all at once.

My hope is that the constant repetition of some of these exclamations will give the reader a sense of familiarity with them, so that their meaning will seem clear. In other cases, I have tried to reflect the tone, if not the exact words used by the speakers. As Pasolini writes in "Roman Slang," "What a Roman admires above all is a person's oratory skill, his linguistic inventiveness, or at least his vivid usage of slang expressions." I have tried to render this bluster, wit, and aggressive posture with English alternatives not specifically defined as slang, which might assign a specific time, location, and social group to them, in order to communicate the attitude of the speaker. Humorous nicknames, extremely popular among *ragazzi*, are also an interesting case. Wherever possible, I have tried to find English equivalents that reflect their double meaning. In these ways, I have attempted as unobtrusively as possible to bring the reader in close proximity to the linguistic world of the characters.

In part, I have been helped by the fact that a few of these expressions, and even more so, the attitude of the Roman *ragazzo* are still very much alive. Despite Pasolini's disappointment with the Americanization of his adopted city, to the outsider, Rome still maintains this popular, rough, and linguistically inventive aspect. In neighborhood markets and pizzerias only slightly removed from the city center, you can hear people calling to each other, insulting each other with some of the same words and spirit that Pasolini so lovingly collected and grafted into his stories. I read these stories while living in Rome, and through them became aware of the manner of speaking of the people around me, in an inverse experience to Pasolini's own. Aspects of this dialect still exist, and through it, one can catch a glimpse of Pasolini's vision of the city of God.

Marina Harss, New York, 2003

EDITOR'S NOTE

Walter Siti is a Professor of Italian Literature at L'Aquila University. His best known works concern Neo-Realist poetry and the twentieth-century novel. He also wrote two novels, *Scuola di nudo*, in 1994, and *Un dolore normale*, in 1999. He is the editor of the complete prose works of Pier Paolo Pasolini for Mondadori and of his poetry for Garzanti.

The stories, essays, articles, and reportages collected in this volume are "Roman" in at least two ways: in the sense that they were written after Pasolini's arrival in Rome (and mostly in the early years after his arrival, when he was metabolizing his encounter with this seductive and shocking city), and in the sense that Rome is their frame of reference. (A partial exception is "Terracina.")

Almost all the stories were published in newspapers and magazines, but this does not help us in classifying and describing them. The distribution of the texts in Pasolini's archive (now at the Gabinetto Vieusseux in Florence) is more illustrative. These files were organized by Pasolini himself with file names written by him. One of them, entitled (*Articles, essays, etc.*) *and Little Roman stories 1950*, contains "Trastevere Boy," "The Drink," "The Passion of the Lupin-Seller," "Chestnuts and Chrysanthemums," and "From Monteverde Down to the Altieri Theater." In these stories the desire to "read into the thoughts" of young people is strongest; they are characterized by a lyrical, introspective tension like such stories from the Friulian period as "The Speakers," and they are shaped as artistic prose.

In another file, entitled *The Ferrobedò (and other notes and stories, some of which were included in "The Ragazzi")* (1950–1951), we find the manuscripts of "The Dogfish," "The Passion of the Lupin-Seller," "Sunday at the Collina Volpi," "Santino on the Beach at Ostia," and "Terracina." These are the most extroverted and narrative stories, in which action and adventure prevail over introspection. The "realist" style is less consciously "artistic." ("The Passion of the Lupin-Seller" is the only story that is in both files, and it represents a midpoint between these two tendencies.)

It should be noted that, while the stories in the first file were conceived from the beginning as autonomous stories, those in the second file form part of a narrative whole, a kind of ur-*Ragazzi* in three parts: "The Ferrobedò," "Li Belli Pischelli," and "Terracina."

"Terracina" is, as we haved pointed out, a special case. It was conceived originally as a digression within the ur-*Ragazzi*: the protagonists, Lucià and Marcè, tired of their messy lives in Rome, decide to escape by going to stay with Marcè's country relatives. The story was probably conceived as a possible ending to the novel, and concludes with the death of Lucià.

In 1950, a literary competition was held in Taranto for an unpublished story with the sea as "protagonist or setting or background." Pasolini submitted "Terracina." The story did not win the competition, but was commended by the jury and an excerpt from it was published the following year in the paper *Voce del Popolo*, in Taranto, in five parts from July 7 to August 4. An editorial note included with the second excerpt pointed out that the "excessive length and crude language render unwise the publication of the full work."

It has been impossible to find the story in the form in which Pasolini sent it to the literary competition; we have presented here the excerpt published in The Roman paper *Il Quotidiano* under the title "Santino on the beach at Ostia" as well as all of the typescript entitled "Terracina," which contains the remaining *Voce del Popolo* excerpts, integrating and completing them. Two of these were slightly reworked by Pasolini for *Il Quotidiano* and were published on April 19 and June 8, 1951, with the titles "Night over the Sea at Terracina" and "Dissolve over the Sea of the Circeo."

The reportages included in this volume are certainly more fragmented and "servile." But underneath a certain routine quality and the superficial verve (worthy of the crime pages), we find the drive to combine emotion and clarity, the attempt to use poetry as a political instrument, which foreshadows Pasolini's later extraordinary journalistic style.

Because of their Roman theme, we have included two drafts of screenplays, *Roman Deaths* and *(Ri)cotta Cheese*, keeping in mind that Pasolini's film drafts were usually a genre unto themselves, a sub-genre of narrative.

We decided to close the book with a 1973 interview in which Pasolini declares his disgust with Rome, which has been rendered unrecognizable by urbanistic destruction and cultural genocide. Here his love story with Rome ends, with the announcement of painful separation.

Let me talk for a moment about the reason we chose the title *Stories of the City of God*. This title can be found in one of Pasolini's manuscripts dating from sometime in the mid-fifties. This manuscript contains a list of possible titles for his Roman works. Beyond the obvious Augustinian connotations, *Voci nella Città di Dio*—Voices from the City of God—is the title of a book by Danilo Dolci, which Pasolini reviewed in 1951. The notion of identifying Rome with the phrase "city of God" is perhaps inspired by the fact that 1950 was a Jubilee year, and is expressed not only in the list of possible titles but also in his wish (expressed in "The Periphery of My Mind") to give this title to his third Roman novel, which he never wrote. Once this project was abandoned, the phrase reappeared in the second chapter of the first section of *A Violent Life*, which is entitled "Night in the City of God."

In two cases ("The Drink," and "The Passion of the Lupin-Seller") we have published the earliest version of the text, because a later version written ten years later seems more calculated. The author augmented the number of phrases in dialect, muting the immediacy and freshness of the story.

The stories contained in this volume were all checked against typescripts, and certain sections that had been eliminated at publication were reintroduced; subtitles added at publication were also eliminated.

The author's inconsistent transcriptions of dialect were also respected.

At the bottom of each piece we have indicated where that piece was first published (or, in the case of unpublished pieces, the folder of the Archive in which it was kept).

In general there is no discrepancy between the date of composition and the date of publication of each text. Because of this, we have only indicated the date of composition in the case of unpublished pieces, or when the piece was published after the death of the author (dates indicated by the author are in parentheses; conjectural dates are in brackets).

Walter Siti, Rome, 1995

STORIES FROM THE CITY OF GOD

PART I

SKETCHES OF ROME

TRASTEVERE BOY

The kid who sells roasted chestnuts at the end of the Ponte Garibaldi gets down to work. He sits in a groove in the parapet of the bridge with a small stove between his legs, looking no one in the face, as if his relationship to the rest of humanity were at an end, or as if he had been reduced to only a hand, not the physical hand of a small boy or an elderly lady, but an abstract hand, a mechanism for accepting payment and delivering merchandise in a rigidly calculated and predetermined exchange. And most likely the young man—he is as dark as a violet, dark as only the boys from Trastevere neighborhood can be—subtracts a few chestnuts from the abstract hand of the customer: one chestnut more on the grille and less in the hand amounts to nothing more than a mathematical calculation, a sum or a subtraction. The customer is an abstract figure, and, morally speaking, the fraud hardly registers.

The dark-skinned boy calculates his two sets of parallel figures—chestnuts and *lire*—with a completely internalized avidity: the trick is destined to succeed. Perhaps even these hours between the afternoon and the evening are an abstraction to him. The evening is nothing less than the moment when the ratio between two contrasting figures reaches its emotional zenith, the moment of truth, conclusive and extraordinary. . . . At that moment (where? On the Via della Paglia? In some neighborhood alley, gloomily perfumed with springtime?) he will calculate his profit.

Will the wolf smile then? With his distracted air, a perfect simulation of the most honest indifference, masking his faulty arithmetic, will that embezzled chestnut make his heart leap with joy like any normal heart? It's a sad truth, but it's preferable for his heart to beat faster for ten *lire* won through trickery than not at all.

In any case, at this moment he is so preoccupied with his calculations that if there were even a flash of another thought in his head, it would appear in his eye only as the faintest shadow. And so, little by little, in the compact, colorless avidity of the eye, a shadow has begun to form; after all, it would be completely unnatural for an eighteen-year-old boy to have no thought for anything but the struggle between two numerical series. True, it is a struggle for survival: but how many and what diverse vocations coexist in the life of a young *Trasteverino*[1]?

For my part, I would like to understand the mechanisms by which the Trastevere—shapeless, pounding, idle—lives inside of him. His eyes are like two sigils: two black wax seals impressed on the gray of his face which emanates no light from within, an opaqueness amply compensated, certainly, by the intense light of the Roman sky. His heart is like a tape-worm that constantly digests innumerable sighs, screams, smiles, and exclamations; which has digested, without its host's knowledge, an entire generation of his peers, young men made of something slightly more than clay, young men who are less than Apollos. . . .

Behind him the Tiber is an abyss drawn on tissue paper.

And one has the hopeless sense that he *does not see it*, as if to him it were something so external as to have no place in his reality. Or as if, like a horse with blinders, he can only see a small portion of it, determined by the strictly functional nature of his reality. Thence the pain; and the pity. With his knees open savagely wide around the small stove and his torso leaning over it, he compresses himself into a circle which no magical formula can break open. The entire length of the Tiber, with its deathly haze over the Tiber Island and its landscape that weighs on the eye, the domes light as veils

---

[1] A person from the neighborhood known as the Trastevere, or "beyond the Tiber."

in the wind, bears down on his back with the weight of a child's little finger against the Great Wall of China.

So, Rome does not interest him; *c'est la vie*. His Baedeker is as dangerous as a pistol. The chapter on the Trastevere does not include Santa Maria with its flaccid figures by Cavallini, but instead perhaps the five toughs who were hanging around the intersection of Via della Scala and Via della Lungara last night, drunk with a joy that stank of blood like a butcher's shop. Perhaps it also includes the boy—brown as a statue pulled from the mud of the Tiber—who lingers near the Cinema Reale. What else can be found in this harsh guidebook which reduces Rome to its own obsession? Things perhaps that we civilized types cannot even imagine. A particular, functional segment of the Tiber . . . a functional itinerary through the boy's neighborhood. . . . The chestnut-seller knows much, of that we can be sure; he knows, but he remains silent as the tomb. In order to communicate the topography of his life, he would need to stand outside of it; but where does the Tiber end and the boy begin?

Incredibly, at a certain point he speaks to me. "*A moro*[2]" he says, "what time is it?" If he had stood up and flung the red-hot grille in my face I would not have been more surprised: I believed I was completely external to his functional reality, to those segments, angles, or layers of Rome which I thought were the only things that could leave a mark on his

---

[2] An expression in Roman dialect that means something like "Hey, you," or "Hey, mister."

retina. The fact that I do not own a watch is for him a small sudden explosion of irrationality just as the sight of the shadow in his eyes was for me. But I am quickly swept out of his mind, while for me the mystery has only been slightly transformed, and even intensified. Now his Baedeker threatens to become an undecipherable catalogue: the Trastevere, from the Cinema Reale to the Cinema Fontana . . . a few shows at the Altieri Theatre (where for 50 *lire* you can also watch the variety show) . . . the Via delle Stalle and San Pietro in Montorio, on spring nights. . . .

I hover around the circle created by the boy, but do not enter: the boy's heart, which existed already before the hour which does not appear on my nonexistent watch, has lived too submerged in poverty for too many years.

There is a smell of laundry left to dry on the balconies of the alleyways, of human feces on the little stairway down to the water, of asphalt warmed by the spring air, but the boy's heart appears and disappears on the side of the Stazione Trastevere or on the 129 bus, so distant that poverty and beauty are one and the same.

Il Mattino d'Italia, Rome, June 5, 1950.

THE DRINK

The floating platform was almost empty at that hour. There were just a few office workers who would be gone by 3.

Then, the real customers started to wander down from the Ponte Garibaldi and the Ponte Sisto. After half an hour, the patch of sand between the embankment and the floating platform was as busy as an ant-hill. *Nando*[3] was sitting on the swing, his back to me. He was about ten years old, scrawny and misshapen, with a large tuft of blond hair above his narrow face, on which a large mouth smiled brightly.

He watched me out of the corner of his eye. I went over and asked him: "Would you like a push?"

He nodded, joyfully, grinning more widely than ever.

---

[3] Abbreviation of the name Fernando.

"Get ready! I'm going to make you go really high!" I warned him, smiling.

"That's okay," he answered. I sent him flying, and he yelled to the other little boys: "*A maschi*!⁴ look how high I am!"

After about five minutes he was on the swing again, and this time he didn't keep quiet. "*Moro,*" he said, "will you give me a push?"

He got off the swing, but continued to hang around me. I asked him his name.

His shoulders were burned, as if by a fever rather than by the sun. He told me they stung. By now Orazio's floating platform was a merry-go-round of people: some lifted weights, others did chin-ups, others stripped their clothes off or just lazed around. People yelled at each other, sarcastic, arrogant, and relaxed. A group went over to the diving board and started jumping in, doing cannonballs, falling into the water, somersaulting. I went over to swim, under the pylons of the Ponte Sisto. After half an hour, back on the sand, I saw Nando, gripping the side of the platform; he was yelling over to me.

"Hey!" he said to me, "do you know how to row a boat?"

"Sort of," I answered. He turned to the lifeguard. "How much?" he asked. The lifeguard didn't even lift his head: he leaned over the water as if he were talking to it, and he was clearly in no mood to joke around:

---

⁴ Phrase in Roman dialect, from "maschio," or man, that means something like "Hey, guys!"

"One-hundred and fifty *lire* for an hour, two people."

"Yikes!" Nando blurted, his little face still beaming. Then he disappeared into the dressing rooms. He reappeared next to me on the sand, like an old friend.

"I have a hundred," he said.

"Lucky you," I answered, "I'm completely in the red." He didn't understand. "What does that mean?" he asked.

"I'm broke," I explained.

"Why? Don't you work?"

"Nope." "I thought you had a job," he said. "I'm a student," I said, to simplify matters. "Don't you get paid?" "Actually, *I* pay." "Do you know how to swim?" he asked. "Yes, do you?" "No, I'm too scared. I only go in the water up to here!"

"Shall we go for a dip?" He nodded and followed me like a puppy.

When we were near the diving board, I pulled my bathing cap out of the pocket of my swimming trunks. "What is *that*?" he asked, pointing at it.

"A bathing cap," I answered.

"How much did it cost?"

"I paid four hundred *lire* for it, three years ago."

"I love it!" he said, putting it on. "We're poor, but if we were rich my mother would buy me one of those."

"You're poor?"

"Yes, we live in one of those shacks on the Via Casilina."[5]

---

[5] The shantytowns on the Via Casilina appear in many of Pasolini's literary and film works.

"So how come you have one hundred *lire*?"

"I made it carrying luggage."

"Where?"

"At the station." He was a bit reticent; perhaps he was lying. Perhaps he had begged for it. Those little arms of his could hardly have carried a suitcase. I took the bathing cap back, patted his tuft of hair, and asked: "Do you go to school?"

"Yes, I'm in the second grade . . . I'm twelve years old, but I was sick for five years . . . Aren't you getting in?"

"Yes, I'm going to dive in."

"Do an angel dive," he yelled as I balanced on the diving board. I did a normal dive, swam a little, and clambered back to shore through the weeds, muck, and garbage.

"Why didn't you do an angel dive?" he asked me.

"I don't know, this time I'll try it." I had never done one, but I attempted to just to please him. When I came out again, he was happy. "That was a nice angel dive," he said. In the middle of the Tiber, a young man was rowing upstream in a canoe-like boat. "What's so hard about that?" said Nando. "The lifeguard wouldn't let me take a boat out."

"Have you ever rowed a boat?" I asked. "No, but what's so hard about it?" When the young man reached us, Nando stretched out on the diving board and started to yell at the top of his lungs, his hands cupped around his mouth: "*A moro, a moro*, can I get on with you?" The man didn't even answer him. So Nando, still smiling, came back towards me. At that moment, some friends of mine came by and I joined them. I watched them play a game of cards at the bar on the platform.

Nando reappeared, holding a copy of a newspaper, *L'Europeo*.

"Here," he said. "Read it. It's mine."

I took it, just to make him happy, and started to leaf through it. But Orazio came over and grabbed it out of my hands without a word and started reading it, annoyed: it had been a joke. I laughed, and went back to watching the game. Nando came up to the counter.

"I've got one hundred *lire*," he said to the lifeguard. "What can I buy?"

"Orange soda, beer, soda pop," he answered, blankly.

"How much for a soda pop?" Nando asked.

"Forty *lire*."

"Give me two."

A moment later I felt a tap on my shoulder, and there was Nando holding out a bottle of soda pop. I got a lump in my throat, so that I could hardly find the voice to thank him, or say anything at all: I swallowed the drink and said to Nando: "Will you be here Monday or Tuesday?"

"Yes," he answered.

"So next time it's on me," I said, "and we'll go for a boat ride."

"Will you be here Monday?" he asked.

"I'm not sure; I might have to go out with some friends."

Nando counted the money he had left. "I have twenty-two *lire*," he said. He stood there, lost in thought, staring at the price list with his happy face. I wanted to help him in some way.

"What can I buy for twenty *lire*?" he asked the lifeguard.

"Keep your money," he answered. "Look," I said, "the seltzer water costs ten *lire* a glass."

"It's warm," said the lifeguard.

"What can I buy for twenty *lire*?" Nando repeated.

Then he turned to the lifeguard: "So what? Give us two glasses." The lifeguard poured two glasses, and Nando said to me: "Drink." He had paid for a second round of drinks.

"So if you don't go out with your friends, will you come on Monday?" he asked me.

"Absolutely! And you'll see, we'll have a good time." Then he decided to go on the swings again; I pushed him so hard he yelled down to me, laughing: "Stop! My head's spinning!"

Night fell, and we said our good-byes.

Now I can't wait for Tuesday, so I can show Nando a good time; I have no job, no money, but after all Nando only had those 100 *lire*. Millionaires, like the lifeguard on Orazio's floating platform, have no imagination.

"La bibita," *Il Quotidiano*, Rome, June 25, 1950; subsequently published, with variations and under the title "Biciclettone," in *Racconti nuovi, gli scrittori italiani per I nuovi lettori: I ragazzi e I giovani d'oggi*, edited by D. Rinaldi and L. Sbrana, Editori Riuniti: Pionere, Rome, December 1960, pp. 159–163.

THE DOGFISH[6]

Romolé[7] careened into the city marketplace. He was pedaling hard, staring straight ahead without looking right or left; he had decided that if a cop yelled at him to show his permit, he would pretend not to hear. A man with a clear conscience—in other words, a vendor with a permit in his pocket—would be the last person to imagine that a cop was calling him rather than someone else.

The cop said nothing, and Romolé pedaled through the market, which was scalding under the sun. He headed straight

---

[6] This story, as well as "Santino on the Beach at Ostia," "Terracina," and "Ricetto Remembers," was originally meant to be included in Pasolini's novel *The Ragazzi*.

[7] In Roman dialect, it is typical to abbreviate people's names. Romolé is the abbreviation of the diminutive (Romoletto) of the name Romolo.

for the fish section. There was a lot of activity over there. Amid the chaos, the vendors waited for their customers, surrounded by crates full of fish.

Romolé circled, circled calmly.

He was in good form; he could feel in his heart that things would go well for him that morning.

He sidled up to a stand.

Among the crates, in the last row, there was one that contained two large cod. He picked one up, lifted up its gills to see if it was fresh, and held it against his nose to really get a good whiff; in other words, he went through all the motions. He squeezed and sniffed the two cod and then put them back in their crate. Then he pulled the crate back by about twenty centimeters and stood in front of it, still messing about fastidiously. Then he gave the crate a kick with the heel of his shoe and sent it flying into the middle of the floor.

Combing the tuft of blond hair which came down almost to his nose, he walked toward the scale, calmly, as if he were a fishmonger preparing to make a purchase, just to see if anyone had noticed the kick.

So far, so good. He went over to the case with the two cod and dropped a receipt into it. Then he picked it up, quite openly, and walked off with it under his arm. Once he was outside the area of the fish vendors, he put it in a wheelbarrow that belonged to a fishmonger friend of his. He paid his friend fifty *lire* up front.

Then he headed back into the fish market.

He went around two more times, checking out the merchandise at the other stands. The crowd and confusion had increased. The morning sun was boiling hot.

Then Romoletto noticed the dogfish. It was a big fish, and must have weighed about 15 or 20 kilos. He stared at it, openly, and immediately noticed that it wasn't fresh. He walked confidently over to look at some fish on the other side of the line of cases and then doubled back, grabbed the dogfish, and walked off slowly with it under his arm.

Someone else was using the wheelbarrow, so he stashed the dogfish in a corner near the back of the market. A cop came into the fish market to take a look around, and Romoletto walked away, whistling. He fetched his bicycle, wrapped the cod in paper and tied the package to the bicycle seat with string, hiding it as best he could. Then he went back into the fish market. The cop was still there, but Romoletto calmly picked up the dogfish and walked right by him with it under his arm, whistling. He whistled nonchalantly, but his heart was beating hard, and all he could think about was how he was going to get out of the market without showing a permit. It would be more difficult now, with the goods. Just at that moment someone walked by with a wheelbarrow. Romoletto dropped the dogfish into the wheelbarrow and followed on his bicycle. Ten minutes later, the cod, the dogfish, and he were outside. He picked up the dogfish, tied it to the bicycle seat along with the cod, and took off. He pedaled fast, feeling happy. It was late morning, the air was hot, and the

Testaccio neighborhood market would be crawling with
people. After a quarter of an hour he was at the market. The
fishmongers were packing up for the day, so he had to
hurry. Romolé ran over to one of them who was closing up
shop, a friend of his, and asked to borrow a table. He bought
two bunches of leaves, and set up shop.

The two cod went in the blink of an eye.

They were nice big fish, about two-and-a-half kilos each,
and Romolé got 1,200 *lire* for them. Now there was just the
dogfish to unload.

Romolé had high hopes for the dogfish. He peeled it, never
doubting that it would be red on the inside.

In fact, it was black, black as pitch, and it reeked of ammonia. Romolé ran his fingers through his hair. He was
tempted to throw it away: he didn't want to have it on his
conscience; whoever ate that fish was taking his life into his
hands. But he needed the money. He brought down the price;
after all, dogfish was a fairly obscure fish, and people didn't
know what it was supposed to look like.

But even at the lower price no one bought the fish. They
came over, caught a whiff, and turned away.

Romolé was feeling even blacker than the fish. Then he
had an idea. He ran over to a lamb vendor, bought two por-
tions of blood, and put them in his handkerchief. Then he
squeezed the blood through the handkerchief and spread
it over the fish, painting it bright red. He worked carefully,
scrubbing the creases and folds on its belly. When he was
done, the dogfish was flaming red, fresh as a rose.

Romolé cut it in half and placed the pieces on a lovely green bed of leaves.

But what about the stink? Now, people came up to look at the bright red fish, but as soon as they caught a whiff of the ammonia smell they turned away.

"Get your beautiful dogfish!" Romoletto yelled. It was beautiful, but it reeked. He had another idea. He ran over and bought two old lemons and started to scrub the dogfish all over, all the way to the backbone. Until the stink was gone.

Now Romolé could yell as much as he liked.

"Get your beautiful dogfish!" he yelled, "get your dogfish for just 400 *lire*! Take a look at this beauty! I'm giving you pure gold, I am! Get your dogfish for 400 *lire*!"

People started to come over, and someone bought a piece. Romolé sold 100 grams right away. The news traveled fast around the market, and people started to crowd around. After half an hour the dogfish was gone. Romolé gave 100 *lire* to the young man who had lent him the table and beat it out of there, heading for the *Trastevere*.

La libertà d'Italia, Rome, September 20, 1950.

THE PASSION OF THE LUPIN-SELLER[8]

Three o'clock, the Campo dei Fiori. Morbidone[9] stood under the rain, which cooled the stench of squalor. His back was against the blackened corner of a building, and he waited for the time to pass: the shutters of the Borgia cinema were still closed. He tired of standing still, kicked a banana peel, pulled himself up, and nonchalantly walked toward the statue of Giordano Bruno, which glistened in the rain. Some children were playing marbles. A group of little girls ran by, carrying red umbrellas.

---

[8] Salted lupin seeds were often sold in Italy in paper cones as a snack. They are now rare, except in some southern cities like Naples.

[9] It is typical in Roman jargon to give people nicknames. "Morbidone" could be translated as "Softy."

How quiet it was! As slowly as the half hour that hesitated to pass, the rain rustled against the paving stones, exposing a combination of smells: anvils, dirty interiors, wet bed sheets. Morbidone's expression was darker than the sky, which in the meantime had begun to clear. The Borgia's shutters were raised with a crash at a few minutes before four o'clock; by that time an eager crowd had formed, and the sky was almost completely clear, its color a pale blue as tender as milk.

A few light clouds had run aground atop the façades of the dark buildings. Above the Palazzo Farnese, the sky was a fan of shadows.

Morbidone peered into the semi-darkened windows of a shop; it looked like a bedroom in the early morning, with the beds still unmade. But suddenly, what splendor! With his hands in his pockets, his tuft of black hair stuck to his forehead, olive-colored cheeks streaked with water, and eyes shining . . . Morbidone had fallen into a trance, gazing upon this wonder of the Campo dei Fiori.

It was a sky-blue sweater. The sweater was large, meant for a boxer's frame. Wide at the shoulders and chest, like a seascape, narrow at the waist. And the color! It was a light blue, both discreet and subtly alight. It would have been blinding in the sun on the Campo dei Fiori.

A wide yellow stripe divided the sweater into two vast areas, from the neck to the waist. Two equally yellow, but narrower stripes ran down the outside of the sleeves.

It was hanging on a hook in the middle of the shop window, as if standing guard, open wide, and its beauty obscured everything around it. Morbidone pulled himself away with a sigh; he walked back and forth in the Campo dei Fiori, paused in front of the newspaper stand, and bumped into Cravatta[10] and Remo, who were off to the Piazza del Popolo, to sell bottles of perfume. But he could not stop thinking about the blue sweater.

He went back to the shop window to gaze at it. It was truly a marvel. "*Ammazzalo*,"[11] he mumbled to himself, "Talk about the seven wonders of the world!" With the same dark look in his eye, he stepped into the shop and asked the old lady how much it cost.

"Six thousand *lire*," she said.

A few minutes later, the cinema opened. The housemaids, children, and young men who had been waiting outside rushed in and took their seats in the cinema which, half empty, echoed with their loud exclamations. Some of them smoked, their legs draped over the seat in front of them; others poked and shoved their friends. Morbidone picked up his tray and started to go up and down the aisles in the dark, dank cinema.

That night, the sky was completely clear. The stars were shining. The aroma of wet hedges floated down from Villa Sciarra and the Janiculum Hill,[12] and the Tiber gleamed as it flowed under the glint of the stars.

---

[10] Nickname which means "tie."

[11] Literally, "Kill it!", but it is a word in Roman dialect that expresses surprise or wonder, like "Holy shit!"

[12] A hill in Rome, behind the Vatican, once the location of working-class neighborhoods.

Half asleep, Morbidone boarded the #13 tram, relaxed on the seat with his hands in his pockets, and was finally able to focus his thoughts completely on the blue sweater. The sweater enveloped his chest, magically doubling its strength and breadth. The boxing match had just ended and Morbidone had knocked out his opponent. He was wearing the sky-blue sweater, and the eyes of his pals gleamed with envy, especially Luciano and Gustarè.[13] They went out into the street, and every girl had eyes only for him.

And then it was Sunday, at the beach at Ostia, or no, at the soccer game. The Roma team would win—to hell with Luciano and Gustarè—and he would wear his blue sweater and go dancing at the Trionfale, where his cousins went; he would dance with the most beautiful girls. The dream came to an abrupt end at the last stop on the tram line.

In the Donna Olimpia neighborhood, everyone knows everybody else. It's like a small town. On his way home, he saw Luciano and Zagaja, who were talking about the game. He stayed out late with them. When he got home, his father had been waiting up for him, and the two of them got into a fight. His father hit him. Morbidone went to bed and decided that he would leave home the next day. He had seven hundred *lire* saved up.

By the following morning he had changed his mind: the seven hundred *lire* would be the first payment on the six thousand he needed in order to buy the sweater. But his

---

[13] Gustarè is the abbreviation of the name Augustarello.

passion for the sweater had poisoned him. At noon he had
another fight with his father, and so he decided to leave home
once and for all. He would buy the sweater all the same, even
if he had to steal for the money. The weather was beautiful
again, almost as beautiful as it had been in August. There
were people bathing in the river. "Good thing, too," said the
lupin-seller, "if I'm going to be sleeping under the stars."
He went to work at the Borgia, and finished late. He didn't
take the #13 tram, and didn't return to Donna Olimpia. He
found that he could daydream better as he walked. With the
blue sweater in his heart, Morbidone slowly climbed the
Janiculum hill and found a bench to stretch out on. But it
was difficult to sleep on the hard surface! The splendid blue
of the sweater kept him company in the shadow of the trees;
through the leaves he could see the stars, and then the moon
began to shine, in a golden halo.

Morbidone shivered from the cold, and sleep fell heavily
over his chilled body. He awoke very early, when the sun was
just showing over the horizon, infusing Rome with a dazed
pallor. Two young men, wearing gray sweaters, blue pants
with elastic around the ankles, and athletic shoes appeared
on the deserted Janiculum. They started jumping up and
down, punching the air, and running around the square.
Morbidone watched them as they exercised, and when they
started to walk down the hill, he followed.

The Campo dei Fiori was a circus: colors and exclamations
flashing under the already burning sun. People yelled, pro-
tested, declaimed their wares; wheelbarrows, bicycles, and

trucks crossed paths, in a festival atmosphere. Morbidone stole some fruit and ate it. Then he went to the shop window to gaze tenderly at his beloved.

"Il Popolo di Roma," October 18, 1950; published later, with changes, under the title "Il Cartina," in *Galleria Colonna*, Rome, I, n. I, October 13, 1960.

DELIRIOUS ROME

Two cold sparks shot out from the antennas of the FR and FL trams as they crossed on the Via del Mare, one the color of grenadine, the other of a mint ice. For a moment, two phosphorescent shadows gleamed against the asphalt, sweeping over the throng of waiting passengers like the wing of a blind angel.

The two phantoms, one scarlet and one emerald green, were rendered geometrical by the marvelously Euclidean air of the Via del Mare, where the ruins, illuminated by reflectors, wallowed in empty space with an air of comfort, amplitude, and equilibrium that seemed more celestial than geometric. They met at a precise moment which was fixed by the arms of the clock: September 14, 1950, 9:05 PM.

The commuters traveling toward Porta Metronia or the
Piazzale Flaminio, whose identities have been extinguished
in the normal course of business and human contact by an
unthinkable excess of presence, actuality, and nature, calmly
perceived the presence of the two electric beings which had
fulminated them at that precise, abstract moment of their
lives: "9:05 PM, a night in 1950." They were only slightly
brighter than the reflectors that bathed the arches, buttresses,
and colonnades in a pool of sterilized light. These were ele-
mental colors, pure tints extracted from the rainbow by an
optical illusionist for his experiments, spirits iridescent as
soda pop, shooting over the Chagallian composition of passengers, trolley buses, and ruins; a flash of Bonichian[14] mag-
nesium which reduced the space to cubes, spheres, etc . . . a
masterpiece of enchanting, abstract hypotheses. Five minutes pass . . . not more than five minutes . . . and now the chill
of those two angelic shudders, red and green, has been absorbed without a trace by the Via del Mare. In five minutes,
it has aged, blindly chasing time, immersed in a new, unthinkable, mortal present.

*

The Forum, an enormous sequence marked by a slowness
that borders on fixedness, is blasted by a sun which does not

---

[14] Gino Bonichi (1904–33), was a painter who founded the Roman School, an
expressionist movement (ex. *The Roman Courtesan*, 1930).

even produce warmth, a morning sun still slightly tinged with a fragrance of cabbage—fragile, ardent, vaporous. The pale, smoky red to rust-yellow-colored air, furrowed by the rays of light, like a provincial parlor in the early morning, while the maids dust the furniture; or like a late baroque drawing, perhaps with a greenish-pink hue above the sepia and green markings of the pen, introduces an element of romantic, meteorological disorder, between the intent gazes of the tourists and the piled, scattered stones below. . . .

The anthill is deserted.

But in the purity of this day, the stupendous traveling shot of panoramic views ends at the side of the Campidoglio, soaked in sunlight, spraying sun, hardened under the sun: Gogol, Goethe, Stendhal, Seneca, Gide . . . what florid prose! The onlooker's eyelashes are dried out by the light, his stomach acidic, and his fingers swollen: but the surface of the brain is exposed like a negative by the perfect, fragmented architecture. . . .

*

Workmen, their souls more closely woven than their Sunday trousers, merchants and elderly shopkeepers: faces, rendered stupid by good health. There are 35 thousand of them in the stadium. They exhale their *romanesco*[15] with

---

[15] A combination of accent, vocabulary, and expressions that make up the Roman dialect.

collective sighs as powerful as roars. This is their obsession. A small red aircraft weaves elliptically around the stadium, dragging a huge banner, flapping in the wind, advertising Linetti brilliantine. All these potential inhabitants of the Regina Coeli prison, gray as cheap fabric, and as beautiful as suns, carry their yellow-and-red[16] team books in their pockets. These are the same people who at the age of twelve scrawled obscenities on the walls, thus sublimating their deadly exaltation.

Time is pulverized like odorless naphthalene, a greenish veil over the only slightly brighter rough, fresh green of the trees along the *Lungotevere*,[17] above the yellow-red of the water's surface, and the first colors of the evening streaking down here and there from the bitter, dazed sky; it disappears into thin air with a slight puff of air. You hear someone say "okay," see a fragment of a Camel, yellow paper blowing around in the breeze at a street corner, a cabbage leaf rolling around the sidewalk, and that Roman night in 1947 returns to you bathed in a vague odor of fennel and rocket. The trees along the Tiber, their delicate green covering dissolved by the sensual, fossilized, and oily vibrations of light, tremble again in an authentic breeze, in the body of the breeze that the Sunday afternoon weather reports have captured and filed away at birth, fresh as algae, in the Central Apennines or the Tyrrhenian Sea, the origin of long, wondrous meteo-

---

[16] The colors of the Roma football team.

[17] The *Lungotevere* are the streets that run along the Tiber River in Rome.

rological concatenations leading toward Russia, the Baltic, and Sirte. Thousands of percussion instruments breathed, moaned, and laughed, beyond the light blue and lilac colored incrustations of the Roman landscape, beyond urban views as intense as flower beds beneath the Pincio or the Janiculum hill, around archeological remains or distant volcanoes, behind the torturous, baroque, oiled and marble-like instants, beyond rows of peripheral plants with the odor of earthenware pots and small gardens blackened by saltpeter and solitude, behind the sky-blue curves of a festive, communal Tiber; among the sighs, and shouts, and laughter (sometimes nearby, at other times vertiginously far away, from other, even more joyful neighborhoods) the Roman youths, still adolescents, laughed as they walked along the river, their cheeks caressed by the vivid evening breeze.

La Libertà d'Italia, Rome, January 9, 1951. "Squarci di notti romane" ("Excerpts from Roman Nights"), in *Alí degli Occhi Azzurri* (*Alì of the Blue Eyes*), Garzanti, Rome 1965. The original text that appeared in the newspaper has sections that were eliminated in the version that appeared in the book.

SUNDAY AT THE COLLINA VOLPI

"I've got a ball," Agnolo[18] told his friends on Saturday night. "And tomorrow is going to be a nice day." And that Sunday morning a splendid sky, in which even the light veil of clouds glowed, spread over Rome.

Agnolo came down from Monteverde[19] on his motorbike, with his father. Fabbrí,[20] Alfredino and the others came, some of them on foot, some on their bicycles. They met at the Collina Volpi[21] football field just as the sun was starting to come down hard. The president of the soccer club was there

---

[18] Agnolo is a character in *The Ragazzi*.
[19] A neighborhood that lies behind the Janiculum hill.
[20] Abbreviation of Fabbrizio.
[21] Collina Volpi is the name of a street in Southern Rome in a popular neighborhood called La Garbatella.

with his gray car and his stiff shoulders, killing time with the coach. The players stripped off their clothes near the fence at the end of the playing field; the field was suspended like a terrace above the houses and construction sites and the tops of the pine trees. They threw their clothes in a pile near the club president's car. Agnolo was the first one ready, and he dribbled the ball to the middle of the field. Their opponents, the Collina Volpi players, had much older equipment; their blue T-shirts were worn thin with sweat and their sneakers were ragged. But they were older. "Look at them, they could be our dads," said Fabbrí. One of them, a short guy, was about 22 years old and hairy, cheerful, and round as a ball. He teased the kids from Monteverde like an older brother. Agnolo had light reddish hair. His eyes hardened, became like shards of glass as he listened to the short guy, but he said nothing. He turned with exaggerated indifference toward Gino: "Did you see Jolanda this morning?" Gino finished tying his shoelace before answering.

"Yeah, I saw her."

"Where was she?" asked Agnolo.

"At Villa Sciarra.[22] We went as far as the Janiculum together.

"So what'd she say?"

"She didn't say anything."

"What about Luciana?"

---

[22] A park in the Trastevere neighborhood.

Gino started to laugh. "She was lost in her thoughts, that one!"

"Did she believe you?"

"You should have seen it! She turned completely pale. At first she talked and talked, then she shut up completely, she didn't say a word. They all believed it. Even Giannino, he was there too."

"*Ammazzalo*," said Agnolo.

"What, you playing on the left?" Alfredino yelled to him.

"This is where they put me," answered the redhead.

"Our bosses are shits, and you're an even bigger one, 'cause you voted for them."

The team president watched the boys as they got ready. The others were almost all on the other end of the field, taking turns shooting at goal.

Fabbrí, Alfredino, and two or three others were on the bench. Maybe they would play in the second half of the game. They felt humiliated, but pretended not to care, chewing their gum as they sat there in their shorts, with their lovely sky-blue team shirts. "Hey Giannino!" yelled Alfredino, from the bench, across the field. "Aww, shut up," said Giannino as he did squats, annoyed.

Alfredino said to Fabbrí: "His leg hurts so bad he can't hardly move it. And he don't say nothin' 'cause he don't want them to take him out of the game." And loudly, cupping his hands over his mouth, he yelled over to Giannino, who was crossing: "Go Gianní!"

Alvaro, who at nineteen was the oldest of the bunch, stood off by himself, minding his own business. He didn't feel like listening to the others' snide comments: Alfredino told Agnolo again that Giannino was done for, and Agnolo, lighting a cigarette butt, murmured: "If he's expecting me to pass him the ball, he'd better not hold his breath." Then they laughed some more about the joke they'd played on Luciana.

"What'd you tell her?" Agnolo said again. "Did you tell her I was in the hospital?"

"Yup. With a broken leg."

"And I'm tellin' you, she was white as a sheet," said Alfredino, covering his face with his hands.

"You guys ready, you sons of . . . ?" Giannino yelled, kicking the ball. Behind him, beyond the field, you could see the neighborhood around the San Paolo church turning white under the sun. A sung Mass was plying on the radio in the club.

By half-time, the Monteverde team was down, three to zero. The short guy had scored two of the goals. Alvaro was playing badly. Agnolo felt out of place as a left wing; he and Giannino didn't click; he wandered like a lost shadow on the opponents' side. In the second half Fabbrí and Alfredino got a chance to play, but this hardly changed the course of events. By the end of the match, two more balls had gone into their goal.

The air at noon was on fire, but even so two other small teams came onto the field superbly happy, content to play until two o'clock under that merciless sky. While the new arrivals shot at the goal, the slightly older buddies of the boys from Monteverde, who had tired of teasing their defeated friends as they dressed, walked over to a corner of the field with a ball: they formed a small quadrilateral shape, elastic as a rubber band, and started passing the ball. They kicked the ball with the neck of the foot, so as to keep it moving on the ground, without spin, at high speed. Soon, they were all bathed in sweat, but they didn't want to take their jackets off, or even their woolen jerseys decorated with yellow or black stripes, so as not to alter the casual, jokey tone of their exhibition. They did not want to appear fanatical: but the truth was that they *were* a bit fanatical, playing under that sun, dressed as they were, and their game revealed a loud, threatening joyfulness that abolished any possibility that one might find them comical. Between passes, they chatted. "*Ammazzalo*, Alvaro was slow today," a member of the group said, his dark hair slathered with brilliantine.

"Women," he added, turning around.

"Forget women!" shouted someone else, with a look on his face that fulminated anyone who might want to contradict him. "The guy's a fool."

"*A maschio!*" he shouted to one of the boys; the ball had rolled past the fence, and he wanted one of the boys to kick it back over. As he spoke, he had attempted an audacious and contemptuous heel kick and had missed; the others hadn't paid the least attention to the kick or to the fact that he had missed. The boys, now dressed, were sitting on the dirty grass under the wall, burning hot under the sun.

Fifteen minutes later, the next group of twenty-two boys were left playing on the field, yelling and insulting one another in the suburban silence of the sky, dazed by the midday sun.

Il Popolo di Roma, January 14, 1951.

CHESTNUTS AND CHRYSANTHEMUMS

The chestnuts came from the Campo dei Fiori, and the chrysanthemums from Primavalle.[23] The air was pure and their fragrance cut through it like a blade, under the steps of the church, which was gray, then rusty-red, and white at the top, where it was touched by the sun. But how far Chieti[24] was from here! Here, forgotten, sitting on an old block of stone from the church, with a small stove between his legs, his olive or wood-colored face bent over the dull embers, the boy dreamed in the local dialect of this small city laid out under the sun, between the flanks of the hills. If he stood up, say to put his money in his pocket, you could see that he

---

[23] A working-class suburb of Rome.
[24] A town on the Adriatic coast, in the Abruzzi region, east of Rome.

CHESTNUTS AND CHRYSANTHEMUMS   37

was tall, despite his little farm-boy face, dark and expression-less as a fruit, a strawberry or an apple. His clothes were too small; his trousers stopped above his ankles, or rather just below his knees, and his jacket, its sleeves curved at the elbows and so short that they left most of his wrists uncovered, revealed the creases in the back of his trousers. He leaned over the stove, lifting the pan with the chestnuts on it and stirring the embers, which looked discolored, bleached, and humiliated in the Saturday morning light. Such a fragrance of chestnuts, from Chieti, where they were harvested in the sun, down to the Campo dei Fiori in the early morning. Perhaps, all told, the young chestnut-seller could remember no more than ten autumns, but his existence was so entwined with that fragrance—of chestnuts and embers—that one could not distinguish one from the other. Where did the boy end and the fragrance of his wares begin? One was built in to the other, solid and alive, a single being.

The chrysanthemums emanated their graveyard fragrance, intermingling with that of the chestnuts, like lace thrown over an old, heavy sideboard, or ivy on a tree trunk. Just as the fragrance of the chestnuts was compact, so that of the chrysanthemums blossomed; the first was planted in the air like a column, the second spread out like a mist of feathers. The first stuck to your chest or throat, trusting and desperate; the second penetrated all the way to your gut: who would have believed that such perfidious and delicate chrysanthemums could come from Primavalle? And that they had not grown on a cloud, or in the bare, washed-out sky near San Lorenzo or above the Campo Verano graveyard on the Esquiline Hill? *Belli Capelli*[25] grew them up in Primavalle, in his wet, dirty flowerbeds behind the shacks, looking out toward the countryside, smooth as oil, not a pine tree in sight, so deserted that one wouldn't be surprised to suddenly come across a band of cowboys with guns drawn. The fragrance of those chrysanthemums, the freshness of their atoms, did not contain the absence of the dead, but rather the absence of the living. The ferocious melancholy of Primavalle, up above Rome, almost grazing the sky, its houses like purple, rose, and ash colored boxes in art nouveau style, already crumbling and peeling like ruins. Up there, the sun always seemed veiled by a shadow, like a cloud of mosquitoes or disinfectant, even when it was clear and cheerful, in September or in spring, or when the heat peeled the plaster off the walls in August. Unlike the chestnut-seller, how many autumns, Indian summers, and All Saints' Days lurked in the memory of the old lady from Trastevere who bought her chrysanthemums from *Belli Capelli* when he came down to Rome with his cart? But she is distinct from their perfume. The words she uses to imagine things no longer have the power to re-create them: her old Roman dialect is arid: mere prose, old age.

The southern dialect of the boy from Chieti has also aged in his heart: just see with what avidity he pockets his money

---

[25] A nickname, probably for someone whose last name is Belli, meaning "lovely locks."

and calculates his profit. In his small blue eyes, which sometimes bring to mind the glimmer of a grape, a single thought is solidifying. It will strip away the mystery that surrounds him and transform him into an adult. He gives way to dishonesty with an innocence that for the time being makes it possible to forgive him. Ten or twelve autumns from now he will be like the old flower-seller: it will not be difficult to condemn him. He will so clearly be a man, so miserably so, so tediously so. But ten, twelve, or one hundred autumns from now one thing will remain the same: the fragrance of the chrysanthemums, and of the chestnuts. A constant, fossilized mystery, a guarantee of immutability. The Species will always be able to find its own lost time in that.

La Libertà d'Italia, Rome, April 3, 1951.

FROM MONTEVERDE DOWN TO THE ALTIERI THEATER

He walks down from Monteverde and saunters around the Campidoglio, and finally into the Altieri, followed—as by a sharp wake—by the stench of poverty and police vans that emanates from his clothes. Cutting the air with his smell, he enters the room where healthy men and boys like him cheerfully shake off their weaknesses. Molded from a race which for centuries has internalized the color of ruins and the Tiber, with a face like a Leonardo Cortese before he became "civilized" and hair that would make Marie Antoinette go green with envy, the darkness of the hall coats his temples and the gaunt, glowing, and sun-burned profile of his cheek. He is a Roman king, marvelously young and alive in the depths of his sarcophagus.

That mask of beauty, which disappears into the darkness, gives his face a corpulence which disappears in the light of day, or is only faintly visible; his face is bronzed by a metallic, unhealthy sun, filtered through the dirty clothes hanging outside windows in alleyways, and pressed against walls covered with filth, a sun that feeds only the surface of his flesh, devoured from the inside by vice and malnutrition. What lies underneath the marvelously anonymous order of his sketched, conventional beauty? Certainly, some creatures float above the filth with the grace of a dragonfly in the mud.

But . . . misery settles like dust in an abandoned room; if one takes a step one is engulfed in it. Hidden inside that *ragazzo* are a few April nights, experienced far from the countryside and the sky, within walls against which voices ring out like lilies, with a limpid, sharp clarity that, for just a moment, transforms the Vicolo del Bologna into a field of wheat . . . but, ingrained in the stone, the stink of filth and of dirty laundry warmed by the sun persists, as if it were its soul. This atrociously fragrant April is only a sibling inside the boy just as his Trastevere beauty gilds his face. In reality, the flow of his feelings could, if one stopped to think, produce the same horror as the Lungotevere at night . . . if one were crazy enough to think about such things. . . . But, practically speaking, no one is so unwise, and, under the feverish streetlights, the water flows along with a great shudder for a bloodless, anonymous death. . . .

In the end, the *ragazzo* from Monteverde begins to cry as he sits in the Altieri theater. There is no doubt about it: against his hazelnut eyes, fixed, and seemingly sucked in by the stage, a teardrop distinctly trembles. Onstage, the woman and her son speak in *Romanesco*, and it is true, there is nothing like a *"core de mamma."*[26] And the woman pronounces her s's mawkishly, in dialect; she is hell bent on tearing at the hearts of the public, who watch her with the same admiring absorption with which they would listen to a Sunday sermon, or which a paterfamilias, making an unusually deep pronouncement, would employ to affirm to his neighbors that he has always believed in the existence of a Supreme Being. So it isn't much of a surprise that the *ragazzo* from Monteverde has forgotten the aphrodisiac Aprils of his recent adolescence in side streets and neighborhood movie theaters, darkened with sex, and has rediscovered in himself an ancient but persistent vein of family feeling. The conversion of the criminal son before the tumultuous compassion of the mother, soaked with tears like a freshly washed bedsheet hung out to dry, seems completely believable to the *ragazzo*. (Was the *other class* turning his insides like a soup pot full of watery broth? Rhetoric, like the Lord, moves in mysterious ways. Perhaps both lie in wait in ballerinas' dressing rooms in theaters that show movies and a variety show for fifty *lire*. And, in fact, the ballerinas come out just a few

---

[26] *Core de mamma,* in Roman dialect, means a mother's love. A powerful concept.

moments later; as soon as their rubber band legs appear, the parentheses of virile reflection and all talk about Supreme Being and other "serious" subjects, draws to a close.)

So, the *ragazzo* from Monteverde has cried. And this despite the fact that he has nothing much to get teary about where his mother is concerned, and his father, even less; his father is a thief with nothing to resemble a *core de mamma*, and it is quite likely that at that very moment he has a foot in hell and the other in a brothel, and that all he will leave his son is his stink of poverty. And what about his brothers, elder, and younger? They are all on the other side of the Tiber, trapped in their wolflike hunger, their anonymity marked with such mystery as would make even Giuseppe Belli[27] blush with embarrassment if he returned to life in Babelian postwar Rome. But, where mystery is concerned, the *ragazzo* from Monteverde, with his faintly southern cheekbones, exhaling oil and blood, is not at a disadvantage to his brothers. Why then has he just committed this enormous, unbearable act of ingenuousness; why did he cry at the Altieri? If one were to think about it too much, those tears in the eyes of the wolf would become intolerable. Anything but tears could be expected from his immutable destiny. If at least he had cried out of the hoodlum's soft-heartedness

---

[27] Giuseppe Gioacchino Belli, 1791–1863, Italian poet. Born in Rome into poverty, Belli earned his living as a government clerk. He drew from his knowledge of street life in writing more than two thousand humorous and satirical sonnets, often in Roman dialect. His poetry is noted for its vigorous realism.

. . . but no, he cried out of obedience, stupidly. What can one do? Pick up a hammer and bash in the windows of the first fancy car that drives by the Piazza Colonna? Beat up the first diplomat's wife who, coifed and polished as a bibelot, looks out over the Janiculum to admire the view? A protest is essential. A blood donor, a guerrilla, a missionary. The *ragazzo*'s tears must be abolished. Our world has played a trick on this emblem of mystery, and we should all be eternally ashamed. Luckily, the rubber band legs of the ballerinas have come to save the day.

Laughter, the kind of laughter which emerges directly from the sex, transfigures the *ragazzo* from Monteverde. This is another of the strange ways of the Lord. By now, the theater is boiling over with a mysterious fever, the exultation of sex, which is the most incomprehensible thing in the world. Out of Monteverde, the ghetto, and Piazza Vittorio Emmanuele, life bubbles over, a life as anonymously simple as original sin and as complex.

Their eyes, fixed on the pale thighs of the ballerinas— thighs that evoke sunless boarding houses stuffy with the smell of rancid oil—vibrate with the gluttony of sex, the hook, the wire that locks the eyes of roosters when they are about to tear each other to pieces, with a heedless, prejudicial tension, which appears almost false, but in reality is profoundly authentic. More than gluttony, what emanates is the honor of sex, the practice, the skill: that terrible skill which is always attributable to others, an inimitable figure.

The *ragazzo* from Monteverde lets himself be sucked in by that air that stinks of the chalk that boys use to write obscenities in public toilets.

Folder in the Archive entitled "(Articles, essays, etc.) and Roman stories," 1950.

We placed the story after "Chestnuts and Chrysanthemums" because this is the relative position of the texts in the folder.

SANTINO ON THE BEACH AT OSTIA

The sea was as smooth as a sheet of glass.

Santino wanted to take a raft and row it out to the open sea, but he was alone, and he wasn't a good rower. So he climbed up on the pier; it was falling apart and full of gaps, and he swam in the sections where there were no boards, until he reached the small rotunda at the end. He lay down on the stone with his head hanging over the side just above the water.

The green, transparent, tepid sea swelled and deflated between the poles of the pier, sometimes as heavy as marble, other times light as air. Even though the water was already about two or three yards deep at the rotunda, you could see each grain of sand at the bottom; the sand was soft and clean, an intoxicating carpet for the underwater life. Every so often a crab went by like a nimble violet, or a starfish. Santino was meditating on that beautiful scene, when a small boy appeared under the pier on a raft. "*A maschié*,"[28] Santino called out, "give me a ride?" The little boy said nothing. "Come on!" Santino insisted. "All right," the little boy said, gravely. Santino dove into the water and touched the sand with his hands; then he came up to the surface and pulled himself onto the raft. "Let's go out into the open sea," he said to the boy.

The little boy paddled as hard as he could, but his arms were too weak and the paddles kept coming out of the water between one wave and the next. "Let me try," Santino prodded. The little boy traded seats with him and Santino began to row. "It's not so hard," he said. "My mother told me not to go out too far," the little boy said. "So? We're just going out a hundred yards, that's all."

The beach lay beyond the pier; it appeared as an endless arc from one end of the horizon to the other. The sun carved it out of the air in liquefied colors. The brown sand, the colors of the bathing huts, the polished stripes of the umbrellas, the white blotches of the boats, the plaster of the houses, all were amassed under the sun in an unreal stillness which neither the milling about of the inaudible crowd, the back-and-forth of rafts, the flying overhead of a red airplane, nor the glimmering of the sea could shake. But in that stillness, created by distance, one could feel the overflowing joy of a Sunday afternoon.

---

[28] Diminutive of "*a maschio*." See n. 4.

The raft bobbed indolently in the water, the oars flapping back and forth in the air like broken wings, and Santino began to lose his patience. But he was determined to go as far out as he could. He gazed enviously into the distance, toward the pure blue between the sea and the sky and the sails of the fishing boat. The thought crossed his mind that from over there, the shore must be almost invisible.

Then, almost without warning, a small sailboat, white as a dove, appeared from behind the pier. It sailed smoothly and obliquely, leaning over to one side. Santino stopped rowing and gazed at it. As it approached, it appeared to be flying toward them, and then it went past, almost touching the raft with its hull, painted white. It sailed on, as lightly as it had come, appearing to be an only slightly more material manifestation of the wind, and in a few minutes it was far away, indistinct and tiny in the distance, but still vivid in the veneer of the sea.

Soon it would become a tiny sail lost in the intimacy of the open sea, where the blue was so much deeper and more immutable.

Santino had followed its course in silence, and when the sailboat was gone, he turned to his companion happily and cried out: "Come on, *maschié*, let's go out to sea!" And he started paddling more desperately than ever. The little boy kept looking worriedly towards the beach. "You're not scared are you?" said Santino. "Scared of what?" the little boy responded, offended. "Of the sea," Santino exclaimed. The little boy shrugged his shoulders, with an expression in his timid eyes that seemed to say: "Are you kidding?" Santino was excited. He was starting to paddle more steadily, catching the water, which swelled and deflated under the raft.

Meanwhile, they were moving farther and farther away from the pier. The beach was a confused mass of colors under the gold-colored sun. And Santino was happy to be so isolated out on the water. But he thought it would be even better to jump into the water and find himself all alone, detached from the boat, amid the silent waves. "Here, hold the oars," he yelled at the little boy. And he dove in, swimming toward the open sea.

Warm and light as silk, the sea lifted him up and brought him down again; now that he was immersed in its center, his eyes could embrace it all the way to the distant horizon, as if he were in a small valley among flat hills of water, with the crests against the light and the sides tinted by the transparent shadows. He was inside, immersed, and he could sink fully into those shadows. For a few moments, he felt as if he were in a tub, outside of the world, in a circle of solitude, in a small desert full of melancholy green dunes. The reflections of light were deadened by the wide, flat sides of the waves that descended all the way down to the dark depths. Then, a spirit from within the water, overcome by a calm but continuous orgasm, like the breath of a sleeping man, a spirit whose movement extended to every angle of the sea, rose up from the depths, flustering the surface. He suddenly found himself at the crest of a wave, in the burning light, and he could see the horizon, the sails, and the sun.

An immense expanse of low hills spread around him until it melted in the distance into the buoyant, compact expanse of blue. The sea was becoming repopulated, coming to life. Santino swam toward the open sea, leaving the greatest possible distance between him and the raft. He could see it in the distance, its wooden boards shaken by the movement of the water. And further off, the beach, Ostia, terra firma . . . but this was all very far off in the distance, and as far as he could see, the sea was intent on churning and murmuring to itself.

When he was beginning to get tired, he turned and saw that the raft was truly far away. If he lowered his head, he couldn't even see it. He became a bit frightened; the waves around him, like silent church bells, were the same green, but now they appeared to contain an indeterminate threat. A threat that lay in the depths, as if the spirit that agitated the waters from within had suddenly changed its mood.

Il Quotidiano, Rome, September 11, 1951; signed Paolo Amari.

TERRACINA

From the Circeo[29] on the right, indistinct among the clouds, itself a cloud, distant, isolated, its sharpened points tinted with smoky-blue cinders, down in the semicircle of the beach, detached from the shadows of terra firma and only slightly distinguishable from the sky, forming a long curve beneath the eyes, lined with rows of abandoned bathing huts, running directly into a monumental promontory, lay the sea. It filled all visible space: flat, shimmering, and alive.

Behind the promontory—all stone, topped by a ruined temple, pushing forward against the tide, a granite obelisk, a hundred yards tall and sixty yards wide, solitary between

---

[29] Circeo is a promontory in the Bay of Gaeta, south of Rome, near Terracina. In the *Odyssey*, this is the place where Ulysses is bewitched by Circe.

the land and water—the hills of the next bay hurled themselves toward the horizon. There lay the hills of Gaeta and Sperlonga, lined up like links on a chain, undulating, southern, filtering the horizon to its core in the melancholy, rust-colored distance, where the gray of the sky and the sea mixed together in a dreamlike glare.

From the Circeo to Sperlonga the sea looked like an immense lake, one side closed in by the clouds. They were disorderly, heavy clouds, especially over the Circeo, where they darkened menacingly. There was a gap in the middle, and here and there a strip of sky emerged, light blue or yellow. On the left, over the hills, the sun descended in a fan of rays, like reflectors focused on a single point. The sea glimmered there like a drawn sword. Beyond, clumped on the side of the gray, stony hill, lay Terracina.

One could see all of this from the roof of the house of Marcè's[30] relatives, where they were lying. The tiles were wet because it had rained during the night; Luciano was lying there with his hands under his head, gazing into space. Marcello was almost asleep. The roof was high, and the villa was built on a small elevation in the parcel of land, which was covered in small grapevines, like a spider's web. From up there one could see all around, even if it wasn't terribly comfortable. This made Luciano happy. Unnoticed by Marcè, his gaze caressed the furthest reaches of the horizon, where the sea was simply that, pure sea, without a connection to the shore,

[30] Shortened version of Marcello.

with nothing around it. There, more than anywhere else in the cloudy sky, the sun managed to filter through, coloring the air and water blue. It was going to rain for sure. The clouds over the Circeo were so compact and dark that they had swallowed it up completely, and they were spreading over the light layer of clouds that already covered the entire sky; a cold air had also risen, and seemed about to release the first gelid drops of rain. Lucià would have to detach his gaze from the sea, and interrupt the pleasure he derived from it. It was a well-deserved pleasure; he had already begun to crave it the night before they left Rome, dreaming of a sea just like this, solitary, savage and bare. When they had reached beyond the area of the Castelli Romani[31]—the morning air was a bit sooty, and from up there you could not yet make out the sea—behind Velletri, just as the Via Appia began its descent toward a gray wall of mountains, Lucià had stretched up in his seat to see it. A white haze lay around the base of the mountains, as well as a narrow plain, and they appeared to the eye like the waters of a gulf.

"The sea, the sea!" Lucià had called out. "There it is!"

"*A stronzo*![32] answered Marcè. "That's not the sea! Calm down!"

In Rome and the area of the Castelli, it had been a beautiful, clear morning. They saw a few clouds toward the Circeo,

---

[31] The Castelli Romani is the area of towns in the hills around Rome, the Colli Albani. Castel Gandolfo, the summer residence of the Pope, is located here.

[32] *Stronzo*, or "jerk," can be used with differing levels of aggression; here, it is used jokingly or affectionately by Marcè to mean something like "you idiot!"

after Latina, but they seemed innocuous. The rest of the sky was serene. The night before in the city there had been a violent storm; it had begun to rain just as Lucià and Marcè were walking to the train station from the Villa Borghese to make some money for the trip. They gave up on the idea and headed instead to take shelter around Piazza Vittorio. They were lucky: Marcè was able to score a thousand *lire* and a nearly full packet of Chesterfield cigarettes.

There was thunder and lightning, but by evening, the sky had once again cleared. It was the night before the feast of the Madonna, and there were lamps hanging in the windows, sending rainbow-colored shadows down the side streets; thousands of lamps trembled in the crisp, transparent air, and the façades of many churches were covered in an embroidery of electric lights. When they came out of the movie theater, where they had spent most of the afternoon, Lucià and Marcè were struck by the softness of the breeze, and Lucià, looking up into the sky, cried out happily: "Look at the stars!"

They went to pick up bicycles from a repair shop in Trastevere. "Wait here," Lucià said to Marcè at the end of the Via della Scala, "and don't let him see you." Marcè was nervous, and he said to Lucià: "Be careful, he's a clever one." But Luciano shrugged, glancing over at his friend with disdain. He went into the shop, and there was a crowd of people as usual at that hour. He took two bicycles, one of which had racing handlebars, and gave his real name to the mechanic, who wrote it down on the ledger.

Lucià and Marcè rode around the Trastevere for about half an hour, and then Lucià returned to the shop with one bicycle and paid for it. The shop owner didn't remember that he had taken out two, and he took the money and scratched Luciano's name from the ledger.

Marcè was still waiting on Via della Scala, in a doorway. "So how'd it go?" he asked Lucià. "I'm a genius, didn't you know?" said Lucià, indifferently. "Yeah, right," Marcè chuckled. Now, according to the plan, it was his turn; he would have preferred to ride to Terracina on a single bicycle, but instead, Lucià forced him to go into the shop where, trembling like a leaf, he took out another bicycle under a false name. But it went well, and now they had two bicycles; they went to sleep in a shed near the Trastevere train station, off the Viale Marconi.

At the first light of dawn they awoke and washed in a fountain. The entire neighborhood was still asleep, and in the white sky, they could see the skeleton of the oil storage tank among the smokeless chimneys. They jumped on their bicycles and went up a side street, but as soon as they turned onto the Viale Marconi, which was deserted and pale at that time, they ran into Luciano's father.

They turned to stone, not knowing what to say or do. And Luciano's father stared at them in shock, which quickly turned to fury. He was still a bit drunk from the night before; his face was bright red, and his eyes were bulging.

Suddenly he began to yell, and hurled himself at them, grabbing the handlebars of their bicycles. "Where'd you get these?" he yelled. But Luciano and Marcello had leaped off the bikes and run off toward the shed. Lucià's father, still yelling, walked up the side street and turned onto Viale Marconi, toward his friend's fruit stand.

He leaned the two bicycles against the closed shutters of his friend's shop. The two boys had followed him at a distance; as soon as he went inside, Lucià yelled to Marcè, "Don't move!", ran over to the shop, grabbed the bicycles, and brought them to Marcello. They jumped on and pedaled as hard as they could toward the underpass near the station. The streets were still deserted. But Lucià's father had returned to the door and seen them jump onto the bicycles. "When I catch you, I'll kill you!" he yelled after them; and then he came out with another bicycle and began to chase after them.

"Let's go to the Battaglioni Emme,"[33] yelled Marcè.

They took the underpass, to Via Volpato, and raced off toward the shacks of the Battaglioni Emme where, among kitchen gardens, alleys, and piles of trash, they managed to shake off their pursuer. Then, more calmly, they rode off toward San Giovanni in Laterano and took the road to Terracina.

Now they were at Terracina, and the sea that they had been longing for since they passed Velletri, when the Circeo

---

[33] Battaglioni M, or Battaglioni Mussolini: Marcello is referring to the old barracks that had been employed by the army.

had appeared against the horizon, was still nowhere to be seen.

The town looked as if it had been stuck onto the side of the hill, with its tumbledown towers, criss-crossed with twisting and turning streets like viscera, surrounded by stone retaining walls. This was the upper, old city center of Terracina, but Lucià and Marcè had arrived at the foot of the town on the Via Appia, where it looked like a sub-urb of Rome or Ostia. "Where the fuck is the sea?" yelled Lucià. "Almost there," answered Marcè, and on the left, a large stone spur appeared; on the top, between the clouds, they could see the ruins of a temple. Soon they arrived on a small beach.

The sea spread out before them, mud-colored, streaked here and there by a flash of light. Trapped between the prom-ontory with the temple, known as the "Pisco Montano," and the port, the sea seemed narrow, shut in, limited.

Lucià and Marcè got off their bicycles and walked toward the water. It was calm, fragrant, and gave off a slight rum-bling sound. The Circeo was not visible from there. Against the light, on the clay colored water—it looked greenish fur-ther out—they could see a boat floating on the gleaming water, and the dark figures of fishermen. On the wet sand of the beach lay boats, *falanghe*,[34] fishing rods stuck in the sand, and rusty traps left to dry in the wind.

---

[34] Beams slicked with wax or animal fat, so that the boats could easily slide over them and into the water.

Sitting against a wall separating the beach from the road were seven or eight men and boys in a row; they were all crouched over baskets, working silently and diligently. Lucià moved closer to watch them; they did not even raise their heads from what they were doing. They were working the tangles out of long red ropes, coiling them in the bottom of the baskets. There were thin nylon lines attached to the rope, with a little hook at the end of each line. As the men patiently coiled the long rope, they carefully removed each hook and placed it in a piece of cork attached to the side of the basket.

At the end of the beach, in the shallows, there was a group of fishermen, all of them cheerful, who had just come down to the port. The happiest among them were the young men, some of them with their trousers rolled up to their thighs and barefoot, others wearing rubber boots. There was a boat floating on the brown water a few yards away from the shoal, and some fishermen moved around it. The new arrivals called to them jokingly from the beach, and everybody laughed. Then they all began to pull the boat to shore with a rope; a group of them pushed it from behind, their feet in the water, laughing.

"Now this is the sea," said Marcè, yawning; they were both dead tired and the light of the water dazed them. Lucià, still astride his bicycle, watched the fishermen work, in a trance; none of them lifted their heads.

"These guys can't even see me," he muttered. Marcè, on the other hand, didn't know how to reach his relatives' house. He asked one of the men, who had no idea. He asked another, a cheerful young man with a basket of fish on his head, but he knew even less. Marcè decided that they should walk past the port to a small canal with greenish water, which, at that hour, was almost completely empty of boats. He remembered that the house was on the water, on this side of the Pisco Montano, on the beach. Just beyond the port they could see a few buildings and the rows of deserted bathing huts on the beach, battered by the wind.

The beachfront road was equally deserted, and the small palms and oleanders seemed wild. The road pushed forward, seemingly endless, down the coast. But less than a mile along, at the very edge of the group of small, loosely scattered houses, Marcè recognized the house he was looking for. It was on the side of a small hill which was covered with vineyards. The gate was open. They pushed their bicycles up to the door, and Marcello knocked, but no one was home. The house was empty as a drum. So he started to yell: "Aunt Maria!" as he walked around the little house along a footpath, and rapped on the windows with his knuckles.

"I'm so goddamned hungry I could faint," said Lucià. "You're telling me!" said Marcè, back from his trip around the empty house. Lucià stared at him, "Go to hell," he said. "Eat this!" answered Marcè. "I'm so goddamned hungry," Lucià repeated. He got off his bike and went to inspect the premises. Five minutes later, he was on the roof.

Now, all they had to do was move a few tiles and climb inside. They did so, and lowered themselves into the attic, which was full of potatoes and wheat. From there, they went down the stairs to look for the kitchen.

Some women saw them on the roof, and ran over to the fishing cooperative to warn Maria: "There are thieves at your house!" they yelled, and Aunt Maria ran over, frightened, accompanied by three or four young men, and then she cooked four eggs with butter for the thieves. But she hadn't actually recognized Marcè, who had grown tall in those years. And as for Lucià, all she knew about him was what her nephew had yelled into her deaf ear: "This is my friend! His mother and father died in the war!"

Aunt Maria was not a bad person, but when the other relatives (another aunt and some cousins) returned home for lunch at noon, they were not very welcoming toward their guests. At lunch, in the small dining room that smelled of mildew and cat's pee, they changed the subject when it came to finding them a place to stay in Terracina, or when the boys told them why they had left Rome. The cousins, an accountant and a student, were somewhat sarcastic and apathetic, and no one even hinted at inviting them to stay.

"So, Marcè," said Luciano when they were alone, touching his nose as if to say, "What's up?" Marcè made a face that meant "What do I know?" "I'm out of here," said Lucià. Marcè gestured for him to speak more softly. "They don't want us here," Lucià continued, speaking more softly, and clapping his hands together as if to conclude an affair, "They don't want us, so let's get out of here."

"Just hold on a minute," said Marcè.

"Aren't you going to see Uncle Zocculitte?" asked Aunt Maria as she cleaned up in the kitchen. "Of course!" Marcè answered, looking over at Lucià as if it were a good idea. "Let's go over there right now."

"You'll find him home this time of day," said Zia Maria. They went out and picked up their bicycles, and said goodbye to everyone. "Come back and visit," the aunts said from the doorstep, politely.

Lucià crinkled his brow and made a sound with his tongue against his teeth that meant "*Ma li mortacci vostra.*"[35] "Are we sick of this yet?" he asked as they went out to the road, "Thanks for nothing; hello, how are you, now get lost. Does that seem right to you?" he insisted; he was on a roll. "Get over it," snarled Marcello.

Uncle Zocculitte lived on the Vicolo Rappini, under the Pisco Montano, on the little beach where they had first seen the sea. There were crumbling houses all around, and further along, a little snack bar. Behind an iron crucifix with a bouquet of chrysanthemums lay an alley bordered by fishermen's houses, their front steps covered with ragged fishing nets. Uncle Zocculitte was sixty years old, he lived alone, and Vittorio, his assistant, was about to go off to do his military service. Lucià and Marcè could stay with him.

The very next day they began their life as fishermen; at around ten, after working on the baskets for a while, Uncle

---

35 Roman expression that is literally an insult against someone's dead relatives, and which is used to mean, roughly, "go to hell."

Zocculitte decided it was time to go. Vittorio took the rope and placed it outside the door; then he went to a neighbor's house to borrow a bicycle. They left for Mola, which was about ten miles from Terracina. Vittorio carried the long, heavy hoisting cable. Lucià and Marcè, both on one bicycle, carried the basket. The sky was still menacing, yellow, dirty, and wet, and the scirocco wind was blowing; as it blew, it moistened their skin and clothes. It had rained the night before and everything was still wet.

They quickly reached the Via Appia, by the Ligna River; they could see the two endless yellow stripes disappearing into the distance toward Velletri and Rome, bordered by green trees, farmhouses, and bushes. At Mola they stopped and leaned their bikes against each other so they would stand, and began to fish. Marcè was wearing rubber boots over thick woolen socks, like Vittorio. Lucià watched and learned.

Vittorio went into the dirty, plant-filled water of the Ligna up to his ankles. He held the hoisting cable by one end. At the other end of the cable, where the fine, deep net was attached, there was a smaller rope, the end of which Vittorio gave to Marcè to hold, telling him to go into the water two or three yards further and walk forward, dragging the rope. They began to walk through the mud, slowly, and the net dragged along between them, beneath the surface of the water.

Lucià followed the two of them step by step, as if in a procession. Every so often, Vittorio looked up to check the weather. It was a bit clearer now, and one could make out the color of the Circeo. Around them, the birds were sing-

ing, and in the middle of the river you could hear the gur-
gling of the water as it was displaced by the net; these were
the only two sounds they could hear. Vittorio and Marcè
continued for about half an hour, until they had covered five
hundred yards or so; they could see the bicycles standing by
the road further down. "Let's go back," said Vittorio. First,
he dragged the net out of the water and picked out the
water plants that had gotten caught in it. Lucià moved closer
and saw that the bottom of the net was swollen and alive.
"How much have you got there?" "About twenty pounds,"
Vittorio answered. Then they started back toward where they
had begun. Every so often, they stopped to clean the edge of
the net. When they reached the bicycles, they climbed onto
the bank and poured the forty pounds of crayfish into the
basket.

Back at the Vicolo Rappini toward noon, it was quiet. The
round nets and poles lay on the muddy cobblestones. Every
so often a woman walked by with a terra cotta jar on her head
and, moving aside the old net that served as a curtain across
the doorway, disappeared inside. Dirty children, their grubby
little faces already as rough and rusty as fishermen, played
on the steps, wearing ragged hand-me-downs. Some men
were still working their way through the nets, sitting against
the crumbling walls of their houses with their legs open wide.
The noontime sun gilded the alleyway; it smelled of *fraulini*[36]
soup, with oil and preserves.

---

[36] A local fish, a variety of which is known as "dorade."

Uncle Zocculitte's house consisted of a single room on the ground floor. In the middle of the room there was a double bed that filled three quarters of the space; the black iron headboard was decorated with elaborate spirals. The limited space left over was as packed as the hold of a ship. Between the open door and the wall were piled poles, harpoons, and long, narrow jackets; and in every angle of the house there were old nets, hooks, and wound-up lengths of hemp rope. Two wires hung from the central beam of the ceiling, holding an axle, on which nets were piled. The stove, where the *fraulini* soup was bubbling, stood in front of a small window. As soon as they finished eating, work began again. All of the Vicolo Rappini echoed with sounds, as if it were a single courtyard. Everybody worked, including old men and children, and as they did so, they yelled and talked amongst each other and with their neighbors. They sat leaning over the baskets between their legs in the street. Even the people inside seemed to be outside. Vittorio and Uncle Zocculitte took the baskets they had finished preparing that morning and opened them one by one, leaving the fishing line coiled at the bottom. They removed the hooks from the cork and fastened a crayfish on each one, then placed them on the basket cover. There were one hundred and fifty hooks for each line, and the task took them until four o'clock. Then Vittorio changed and went off to the dance hall. Lucià and Marcè were left to do as they pleased, and they went for a walk near the port; there were boats of different types: rowboats, big trawlers, small trawlers, launches, night-fishing boats, motorboats. Uncle Zocculitte's launch, which he had baptized Mariagrazia, was sitting on the little beach at the end of the Vicolo Rappini, the first beach the boys had seen when they arrived the day before.

That night they went to bed early; they shared the double bed with Uncle Zocculitte, and Vittorio slept on the floor. At one in the morning they got up to go night-fishing.

The sky was dark and covered with heavy clouds, though here and there one could see a few stars. It was so dark out that the sea was barely visible, except for a few flashes. On the other hand, the darkness of the sky magnified the sound of the tide—so fragrant that it filled the night.

The beach was full of lights. The fishermen had lit the lanterns hanging from the hulls of their launches, and they moved about in the circles of light, bending over the *falanghe*, standing up straight, straining their arms against the side of the boats until they slid into the water.

Vittorio lit the lamp on the Mariagrazia; the boat had reached its twenty-third year the previous season. It was still robust, solid, and light in its elegant zinc coating, and inside the boat, everything was in order. They pushed the boat over the *falanghe* until it bobbed up and down in the water.

Uncle Zocculitte started to row outward, toward the Circeo; they couldn't see two yards ahead of them. The sea and sky were a single, impenetrable, cold abyss of shadows. Here and there in the gulf one could make out the points of light of the other boat lanterns, still sparse. At that moment, a brightly lit boat was heading out of the port. But it quickly distanced itself from the shore, and became a small point in the far-off waters of the Circeo.

Uncle Zocculitte rowed while Vittorio and the other two sat at the other end of the boat. They said nothing, and all they could hear was the rubbing of the wood of the oars against the iron of the oar locks, and the great roaring of the sea.

"Are we going far?" Luciano asked Marcello after a bit, with a thin voice. "What do I know?" said Marcè. Uncle Zocculitte and Vittorio said nothing. They changed places.

"Let's go as far as the reef," said Uncle Zocculitte, who was sitting on the *macellaro*.[37] "At the foot of the Circeo," he added. Vittorio and he took turns rowing for almost two hours. The shore seemed terribly far away; there was only the sea all around, almost threatening. But in reality they were not very far from shore; if the moon had been out, Lucià would have been able to see something that looked like an enormous black wall rising before him, blacker than the sky; it was the Circeo with its crags and forests.

At the foot of the Circeo, the boat came to a stop and Vittorio leaned over and stared into the water. "Is this a good spot?" asked Uncle Zocculitte. "Twenty-four," Vittorio responded, "that's good enough." " That's twenty-four fathoms," he explained to Luciano and Marcello. "We're above the reef,"

---

[37] Local dialect word for a bench in a boat.

said Uncle Zocculitte. From under the prow, Vittorio picked up a square piece of cork in which was inserted a pole about half a yard long with a black piece of cloth on the end. He tied the second lantern onto the pole and lit it. "Under here," said Uncle Zoculitte, while Vittorio worked, "lies Quadro."

"What's that?"

"It's an ancient city, buried under the water."

"It's here under the boat?" Lucà asked.

"That's right, churches, houses and all. It was as big as Rome," said Uncle Zocculitte.

Meanwhile, Vittorio had attached one end of a long rope to the bottom of the cork, to which he attached the first line with hooks.

The gulf was filling up with small lights; every boat had put a pole with a lantern out to sea. Vittorio too threw in the lantern on its cork buoy; the cork floated, meandering as if drunk on the surface of the water, while the weight disappeared with a splash into the water, pulling down the rope and the line with the hooks to a depth of twenty-four fathoms. Uncle Zocculitte began to row slowly, while Vittorio, standing at the back of the boat, let the rope sink down into the water, steadying it with his hands. The rope sank along with the nylon strings onto which the crayfish had been hooked. When he was finished with one rope, he tied one end to the end of the next one. There were ten in all, almost a mile of rope, and one thousand five hundred hooks. Uncle Zocculitte moved the boat in slow curves, so that the ropes would land on the sea bottom in a serpentine motion; when they finished the last basket, the lantern bobbed up and down brightly less than a quarter of a mile off. Vittorio tied the last stretch of rope to the hoisting cable, and then tied on a piece of cork with a pole stuck into it (this one without a lantern), and threw it into the sea.

Meanwhile, the moon had begun to shimmer, released from the clouds that covered the hills of Sperlonga. The sky was clear now, and the only clouds were further down, blanched by the moon. The sea, between the Circeo and Sperlonga, was dotted with hundreds of lamps. The side of the Circeo, caressed weakly by the moon, reached up to the stars, deep blue against the dark blue of the sky.

Under the light of the moon, Lucià saw the first fish begin to swim up from the bottom. The boat moved away from the second cork buoy, and Uncle Zocculitte rowed rapidly toward the first, which blazed in the night. Vittorio pulled it onto the boat and turned off the lamp, and then repeated his actions, but in reverse: he started to pull the rope onto the boat, dumping them into the baskets. Lucià and Marcè drew close, anxiously. The rope was coming up with the lines hanging limply and the hooks empty. Then, after twenty or thirty hooks, the first *fraulino* appeared, flapping about. Vittorio pulled it off the hook and threw it into a basket at his feet. Lucià leaned over to look at its shiny stomach glimmering in the moonlight and its pink eyes.

"Here comes the cable with the big hooks," said Vittorio, continuing to work with his hands.

"Just one *fraulino* so far," said Lucià, disappointed, as he watched the fish die in the boat. Vittorio and Uncle Zocculitte said nothing. The cable with the big hooks was emerging from the water, dripping wet and empty. Then suddenly a sea bream appeared, and then another sea bream, big, heavy, and shiny as silver. Then a *schiantaro*,[38] a white bream, and another sea bream, and then a six-pound dogfish. Uncle Zocculitte let go of the oars to come over and watch. Seeing that he was silently satisfied, Lucià exclaimed: "We brought you good luck!"

The ropes continued to emerge, one after another, sometimes empty, sometimes dripping with fish, their scales gleaming in the moonlight. Vittorio's big hands pulled them off and threw them into the boat, where they flopped about. *Variati, palombe, mafroni, coccie, schiamuti, cergne, traci*, and little *fraulini*, white as milk.

It took almost two hours to pull in all the ropes; the last fraulino that fell into the basket glimmered in the sunlight, and the side of the Circeo rose up darkly against the sky and the sea, which were blanched by the daylight.

The Terracina market is a square piazza surrounded by tall white walls, with an iron gate on either side. At seven in

---

[38] A local fish, as are the *variati, palombe, mafroni, coccie, schiamuti, cergne,* and *traci*.

the morning the activity there is already intense. Fishermen arrive panting from the effort of running with baskets on their heads to meet the vans owned by cooperatives from Fondi, Naples, Priverno, and Rome, and by the women of Terracina, whose husbands are artisans and shop owners. They come down from the intricate maze of the old city, which is as tough and cold as the rocks on which it is built, pierced by narrow stairways and steep alleys. They gather in the market, making a commotion. The air is deafening. Marcè and Lucià followed Vittorio with the case of fish on his head. There were 16 pounds of fish that morning, and Vittorio had no problem selling them off at four thousand *lire* per pound, a good price. They had gone there directly from their fishing expedition, just before seven, and had not even had time to pull the boat to shore before running off to market. The fishermen helped each other pull in the boats; it was quicker that way. As the boats arrived, the men who were already on the shore helped pull them onto the beach, first with the rope, and then sliding them over the *falanghe*. Marcè and Lucià pushed from the stern; Marcè was wearing the rubber boots which had become his, and Lucià was in his bare feet and legs. The cold, seething water stung his skin, but Lucià didn't dislike the sensation: he was happy, like the others, and they all joked and laughed as they pulled the boat to shore under the burning sunlight.

It was not even eight o'clock when they returned from the market, their basket empty. As soon as they reached the Vicolo Rappini, they began to prepare the hooked lines once again. They took twelve baskets, ten of their own and two belonging to a neighbor who needed some help, and they went to sit on the little beach at the end of the alley, along the low wall. The light in the empty sky and on the water was blinding, but everything was still soaked from the previous day's rain and the Pisco Montano sparkled in the sun. The boats were still coming in, and every so often the boys got up to help someone pull a boat onto the beach. Then they went back to their task: they had to disentangle the mass of rope and hooks and place the rope neatly into the basket, while detaching the hooks and placing them in the cork. Lucià was still barefoot, and his trousers were still rolled up on his thighs, just below the groin, his skin burned by the salt and the sun. The sun was already high.

After two weeks in Terracina, Lucià and Marcè had learned the trade. If Lucià had trouble with the paddles, or took too long to tie the sail, Marcè would yell, "Come on, slow-poke!" and Lucià would counterattack, "*Chi t'è morto.*"[39] Meanwhile, back at the Vicolo Rappini, they had become friends with everyone; the other boys vied for their attention, and the little ones would look at them and giggle. Some of the older boys would ask them about Rome, which Marcè and Lucià had all but forgotten.

In their free time they danced to records at the house of one of Vittorio's friends; Vittorio had left for his military service. In those two weeks, the sun and the salt had tanned

---

[39] Another version of the Roman insult against someone's dead relatives.

and coarsened Lucià's face, making him look much older, and the trousers that Marcè's rich relatives had handed down to him from one of Marcè's cousins no longer fit him. But the jacket looked nice. Marcè had washed his blue sweater, the one with the yellow stripes. So one Sunday, decked out in their best clothes, they decided to follow Uncle Zocculitte's advice and go to Mass.

That day, all of Terracina was happy: after weeks and weeks, the good weather had returned. The Circeo, the Pisco Montano, the hills of the gulf, the towers of the old town, the water, the air, everything seemed to be sculpted out of crystal.

The passers-by, rich and poor, and dressed in their Sunday best—wearing black, but in no way seeming to contradict the brightness of the air—walked upward toward the beautiful church, chatting cheerfully. Lucià and Marcè, who had not set foot in a church since their First Communion and Confirmation at the church of the Divina Providenza on the day of the Ferrobedò heist, were not unhappy to be there, and actually enjoyed themselves. Then they descended the long, steep road at the foot of the church, surrounded by the smells of lunch and the sounds of the radio, and the crowd of people headed home in long streams. When they arrived at the Vicolo Rappini it was newly washed and silent. They didn't change clothes, but walked to the beach in their fancy getup, and Lucià went off to sit in the boat on the *macellaro*. He turned his back to the shore and stared out at the sea, imagining that he was out there all alone, in the open sea, far from shore, as far out as possible, with only the sky all around.

There was only a small group of boys at the snack bar on the beach, near the alley, and the bar itself was deserted. The floor was wet, and there were a few tables set out here and there in the emptiness. The radio was on, and you could hear it blaring from outside, on the beach, echoing against the Pisco Montano and amid the crumbling houses at the end of the Vicolo Rappini. As it played the notes of an old tango, the sky and the sea seemed even more solid, immaculate and blue, as on a summer day.

Lucià and Marcè went inside, and the others turned toward them, inviting them to join in. One of them broke away from the group and timidly walked over to Marcè: "Want to have a drink with us?" he asked. Lucià and Marcè accepted, a bit stiffly. But after a few glasses of wine, Marcè became more talkative; he was red in the face and vociferous. "Trastevere," he said to his new friends, "You've gotta see it! The women! You wouldn't believe the women." And he told them about Rome on Sunday mornings, walking from Donna Olimpia down to the Trastevere, bumping into people you knew, and about the Noantri[40] Festival in July, and summer nights on the Lungotevere, and swimming in the river or at the beach at Ostia, and about the heists they had pulled off, the people

---

[40] The Noantri—or "we others"—Festival is held in Trastevere in July.

they had blackmailed, all the mischief they got up to. He told them about when they bumped into La Manfrina and that friend she was so jealous of, Nadia, who lived behind Piazza Mastai. They had run into them at about two in the morning at the end of the Via della Lungaretta, in a dark deserted spot. Nadia was fooling around with the guys, but she kept saying, at the top of her lungs, "Don't tell her or she'll kill me!" "Did they give her money?" asked the boys from Terracina. "Of course," answered Lucià, grinning, "She's a real lady." Lucià and Marcè had not actually witnessed these events; they had stayed outside in the street, where they could hear their older friends from the Trastevere laughing with Nadia, while La Manfrina, drunk out of her mind, talked to the others. Their Trastevere friends were all pimps, tricksters, shoplifters: the cream of the neighborhood. Marcè also told them about the time he had gone to Via del Tritone with two guys from the gang, and they had slashed someone's tires. The car had finally come to a stop somewhere down the Corso. The owner had gotten out, leaving his jacket on the driver's seat; Marcè and another guy had come by on a bicycle and stolen the jacket and a briefcase out of the car. "There were twenty thousand *lire* and a gold watch in there," boasted Marcè. Luciano smiled to himself and thought, "*Li mortacci tua!*" It wasn't true about the briefcase, and there had only been four or five thousand *lire* in the jacket. "We were friends with the biggest pimps in Rome."

While Marcè continued to talk to the boys from Terracina, Lucià walked off with his hands in his pockets to look at the boats on the beach; the elegant hull of the Mariagrazia pointed out toward the empty sea. He was afraid to bring up what he was thinking with Marcè. But when they walked toward the alleyway at around one o'clock, he took the plunge: "Hey Marcè," he said, "I really feel like taking the boat out."

"But we go out on the boat every day," Marcè exclaimed.

"But we go fishing," said Lucià, impatiently.

"So?"

"I feel like going out for a ride in the boat just like that, just to go out for a ride in the boat."

"Hey, what do I care? Ask the old man."

"Just for fun, you know?" Lucià concluded.

When they found Uncle Zocculitte, he was singing. He was in the house, singing as he sat on the red floor, his head leaning against the curlicued railing of the bed. Every Sunday morning he sang, and he didn't stop till it was night.

At least the sea was smooth, even if the air wasn't too clear, and Uncle Zocculitte didn't have any objection to letting them take out the boat. So after lunch, the boys ran down the alley to the beach, followed only by the sound of Uncle Zocculitte's singing.

The beach was even more quiet and empty than before. The traps hung between the ends of the rusty poles in the dead calm, and the boats were lined up as if they were sleeping, their blues, reds, and greens eroded by the salt water. There was no one around, and they could hear even the slightest gurgle in the endless motion of the Tyrrhenian Sea, from the very edge of the beach to the furthest points of the gulf and the horizon.

The water was as calm as on a summer day, and blindingly blue.

Lucià took off his jacket and threw it into the boat, and then, with Marcello's help, pushed the boat into the water. It started to bob up and down on its own, as if the wood had come to life, and Lucià jumped over the side and into the boat; Marcello gave him a last push.

"Later, Marcè," said Luciano.

Marcè couldn't believe that Lucià really wanted to go off by himself; he stood there on the beach laughing to himself. "Yeah, later," he answered.

Lucià picked up the oars without tying them to the oarlocks and started to row.

As Uncle Zocculitte had said, the sea was calm, but the wind was more uncertain; you could feel the scirocco wind coming on. After he got past the first few yards where the crests of the waves broke on the sand, Lucià rowed easily. He had promised that he wouldn't go out too far, and he wanted to relax and enjoy his adventure without getting too tired. But as he rowed, he sat looking toward the rear of the boat, and he could see the shore, always the shore, as it receded; he felt that it would never recede enough to disappear from sight.

As the boat went out toward the open sea, the shape of the gulf became clearer in the light of the afternoon. First the beach became distinct from the area around the Pisco Montano, which was buffeted by the sun, then the port opened up around the sleeping masts and cranes, and finally the row of bathing huts on the beach disappeared. Meanwhile, the two arms of the gulf, toward Sperlonga and toward the Circeo, became more and more vast and clear to the eye. And in the middle, Terracina rose up high against the side of the gray mountain, with the sun bearing down on the city and the rocks.

After rowing for an hour, Luciano had covered but a small portion of the distance that Uncle Zocculitte covered in the same period when they went night fishing. Though the Circeo was still far off, its blue color was darker now, and he could distinguish the forests and the white of San Felice at the top.

Tired of facing the shore and frustrated at his slow pace, Lucià decided to raise the sail just as the sun was beginning to go down. He turned the pole around, attached the sail, inserted the mast into the hole in the *macellaro* and raised it. Then he sat down in the rear of the boat, even though it was still rather impractical to do so, and the boat, pushed by the strong winds of the scirocco, headed toward the open sea. On the horizon the water was incandescent, no longer blue as it was behind him, and the Circeo, which loomed larger and larger ahead, was a huge dark blue mass against the light. Very soon he could distinguish the forests from the clearings and the clearings from the rocks, and above, in a shimmering fog, he could make out the bell tower and houses of San Felice. And then he was almost at the foot of the Circeo. Down there, under the water, which the reflection of the Circeo colored violet, was Quadro, the buried city, and the rocks were just beyond. He decided to sail along the edge of the Circeo to the tip of the promontory, and then beyond, up to the very edge of the deserted sea, beyond all borders or limits.

The wind blew more intensely now and the air was misty; the clouds had amassed over the hills of Gaeta, at the extreme edge of the gulf. A still bank of clouds, transparent but heavy, cast a long, gray shadow over the sea. The lovely blue of the early afternoon had begun to turn dark as the wind picked up, and the sea was no longer perfectly smooth and had begun to swell slightly.

Perhaps night was beginning to fall; it was later than Luciano imagined. Perhaps that was why the sea had become leaden and colorless in that part of the gulf where he had never gone before, strange, unknown, indifferent. And it was beginning to get cold, so much so that Luciano put on the jacket, which lay on the bottom of the boat where it had fallen.

But behind him, toward the mainland, the air and the blueness seemed unchanged; perhaps they had become slightly more intense in the crystal light that sculpted them out of the air. Other mountains and hills and plains had appeared, behind and around Terracina and all the way to

Mount Leano,[41] opening up and widening toward the heart of Lazio.[42] It would take him only half an hour to reach the furthest tip of the Circeo, and the scirocco blew harder and more continuously, flattening the surface of the water.

By the time the boat reached the tip of the Circeo, the sun was already very low on the horizon, surrounded by a blurry light like a haze along the boundless line of the sea.

There, the sea had no limit except the reddish, serene sky.

The hills of Gaeta, and further south the peak of the Massico,[43] were hidden by clouds or erased by the night, and beneath them, all the way to the foot of the Circeo, the waters were gray and agitated. Quite suddenly, after two or three tired gusts, the scirocco wind stopped blowing and the sail dropped against the mast. There was not even a whisper of wind. But this didn't last long; just as suddenly as the scirocco had stopped, a southwesterly gale rose. In the bend between the Circeo and the plain, with nothing to hold it back, it had broken free and ran wildly through the dead calm of the water, until finally it struck the boat's sail with a blind blow. It lasted but a moment, and then the sea calmed down, under the again soft and regular gusts of the southwesterly wind.

---

[41] Mountain in Lazio.
[42] Region of Italy that includes Rome and Terracina.
[43] A mountain south of Gaeta.

The sea gathered itself peacefully, as if waiting for the profound calm of the night, waiting to be still and alone.

From the folder in the archive entitled *The Ferrobedò (and other notes and stories, some of which went into* The Ragazzi), 1950–1951.

In a previous version, found in the same folder, the end is a bit different, and reveals more clearly the death of Lucià. It reads:

In the bend between the Circeo and the plain, with nothing to hold it back, it had broken free and ran wildly through the dead calm of the water, until finally it struck the boat's sail with a blind blow. The boat was found overturned the following morning by a trawler. It was drifting along in the boundless sea, above which the moon had just set and which lay deserted and tranquil beneath the first light of day.

RICCETTO REMEMBERS

Earlier they had been joking about the Americans, and now Riccetto joined in happily, casually: "Listen to this one. One day, right?" he began, "it was four in the morning, right? My buddy Agnolo comes over to me and says: 'There's a truck in front of the Case Nove. They say there's some good stuff in there.' So I say: 'All right, let's go see.' So we go over to the Case Nove, and we see two other guys there, right? The two of them climb up, grab a bag, and take off. Then I climb in, and I see two guys sleeping. One guy's over here, and the other guy's over there, right? So I take off my shoes, real quiet like, walk right between the two of them, and pick up a jacket that's hanging over by the office. I come back, and say to Agnolo: 'Those other guys took everything, there's just this jacket here.' So he says 'So throw it down here and let's split.'

So then we go through the pockets, see, and we find forty thousand *lire*, and a gold watch, and two packs of cigarettes to boot!"

Il Napoletano[44] watched him, completely absorbed, and nodded with a tired grin. Then he filled his chest with air, and without changing expression, still staring at Riccetto, he said: "Well, listen to this one!" and then he went on for a quarter of an hour telling the long sordid story of his heist. As soon as he slowed down and took a breath, Riccetto went in for the kill: "One morning not too long ago, right? Three of us, me, Agnolo, and Marcello, we're on Via Torino and we see a car parked over there, a small truck like. So I say to Marcello: 'Go see what's in the car.' He climbs up and cuts open the canvas covering, sticks his head in there, pulls it out again, and climbs down. "Let's get out of here. There's explosives in there." So I say: 'Yeah right, get outta here.' And I say to Agnolo, 'Go see what's in there; this guy's too scared.' He goes over and looks inside, comes back and says: "It's just a bunch of tins!" But I wasn't convinced, so I go over and climb in myself and take one of the tins. We move away from the car, and we're arguing about what could be inside. One guy says it's a bomb, another guy says it's nails, everybody has a theory, right? So we go over to the little park over by Piazza Esedra. We need to find something to open the tin, but we can't find a thing. Then we see a soldier standing over there with his girl; I go up to him, 'cause I see he's got a knife,

---

[44] The nickname means "The Neapolitan."

and he opens the tin for me with the knife. But while he's cutting the tin open, he cuts himself. Then we see it's full of bars of chocolate! Now, there's three of us, and the soldier's hand is cut, so we each take one and give him one. So now we figure if we take it home, we've got to share it right? Agnolo and me, we want to eat it ourselves. But Marcello says: 'I'll give half of it to my mother.' Halfway there, he says: 'Well, a little bit less doesn't matter, and then every tram stop he takes another bite, and when he gets to Donna Olimpia there's none left.'

"The Americans were okay! They were a pain in the ass, but they were useful! But the Polacks are just plain mean, you know what I'm talking about? I remember all the kids outside the barracks, right? There was a little guy there, and he was dressed like an American, a little mascot, right? They called him the Brown-noser, and he worked for the Polacks . . . He comes over to me, and says: 'Riccé, you see that truck over there? The stuff's in there, if you take it we can split it fifty fifty. I say to him: 'Aw, all right, show me the truck.' And he says. 'It's over there. So I go over, take the stuff, carry it away with Righetto's cart, and we go home to split it. So I'm coming over to give the kid his money for telling me where the stuff was, and when I come over the Polack's there too, and he's the owner of the truck. And the kid, the Brown-noser, he doesn't take the money, he just turns to the guy and says: 'That's the one that took the stuff. So this guy gets out of the car, and I take off. We run around Monteverde Novo three times, and he's running after me . . . Finally, the guy, he's got longer legs than me, so he catches up with me, and first he ties me to a lamp post and then he beats the hell outta me. He really gave it to me! Kicked me! Punched me! Hit me with his belt . . ."

Orazio, Roma, VII, no. 3, June, 1955.

Riccetto is a character in *The Ragazzi*, and the second chapter of that book is entitled "Riccetto." The magazine *Orazio* published the Riccetto "pieces" (which sound as if they had been recorded on tape). Pasolini meant to include them in *The Ragazzi*, but cut them in the end, at the request of the editor (see the letter to Livio Garzanti dated May 11, 1955, in *Pier Pasolini's Letters (1955–1975)*, edited by Nico Naldini, Einaudi, Turin, 1988, p. 65).

ROMAN DEATHS

Idea for a Film

Imagine the editor of an important magazine, say *Life* for example, turning to a photographer and saying: "My dear X, I would like you to do a photo spread on Rome; do a good job, because I want to dedicate an entire issue of the magazine to the subject. You have complete liberty to choose your subjects."

The first problem for the photographer is finding a formal theme around which he can arrange so much material. He thinks about it and comes up with an idea. The bridges of Rome, bridges as the nexus of different ways of life in the city, and of life in general. There are twenty-one bridges in

Rome, and as the Tiber weaves through the entire city, this means that there are twenty-one vital points, twenty-one nerve centers, twenty-one stanzas with which to describe different aspects of the city, this city in which life is so complex, in which the social classes are promiscuous and disordered, in which everything is grandiose and baroque, poverty-stricken or rich, and full of sunlight.

Content of the Film

Beyond the formal structure of the film—the twenty-one bridges of Rome—the film also needs a meaning, an internal design. A "magazine spread" on Rome can only be a spread about Rome today. The atmosphere of Rome today is completely different from that seen in Rossellini's *Rome, Open City*: today, hope is gone. Has hope materialized? Has it not materialized? It is difficult to say. In any case, hope is no more, or at least so it seems, at the heart of the city. There is an air of restoration, of apparent, somewhat Americanized, well-being, a blind, unreflective, avid, frenzy of life. Restoration and vitality merge as one. Rome has never been so violently vital. Daily life in Rome is among the most lively in the world. And the most profound aspect of vitality is always death: classical Rome, with its dead, and Giuseppe Belli's papal Rome, beneath the "cool" Rome of today, the pinball machines and the wailing jukeboxes.

The purpose of the photo spread is to reveal this tragic, harsh, Bellian sense of mortality through the illustration of the explosive and joyful vitality of the city.

A Film in Episodes?

Not exactly. There is only one episode: a vertical section of Rome, cut in two by the Tiber, with its chaos of life. This single episode breaks into a thousand smaller episodes. The spread covers as many episodes as possible: at least twenty-one, as there are twenty-one bridges. They are episodes of love, of celebration, of violence, of pure joy, of extravagance, of poverty, of wealth.

Of these episodes, which are told with the greatest liberty of rhythm and duration, six will stand out, pulling the film together. Five will be tragic, and end with a death, a Roman death. The last, conclusive episode, however, will be one of explosive, total generosity, representing a kind of hope.

The Five Principal Episodes

I

It is the early afternoon. A half-empty tram travels down the *Lungotevere*. Its squeaking fills the sun-drenched avenue.

There are a handful of passengers seated on the benches. One of them is a young man, twenty or twenty-five years old, dark-haired, dark-skinned, his face disfigured by his moral and material indigence. He has the look of an old loafer, and at the same time he looks desperate, strange.

The tram comes to a bridge in the middle of the city, which at that hour is almost deserted, bleached white as an ossuary. There is a café next to the tram stop which is also practically empty.

The young man gets off the tram, and lingers for a moment in the sun, his face inexpressive and contorted. Then he steps into the café. He must be a regular, someone who is known in the neighborhood. The *barista*, who is more or less the same age, is a friend of his. He orders a cappuccino, and as he waits and drinks his coffee, he talks to the *barista*. Their conversation is spare, allusive, almost as if it were in jargon. It is apparent that the two of them have been companions in adventure, two "*ragazzi di vita*"[45] but the *barista* (not out of moral fortitude, but constrained by objective need) has, as they say, screwed his head back on his shoulders, and decided to work for his living. The new police chief, and the new police tactics he has put into place, are no joke. Our young man, whose nickname is "*Er Muchetta*," has continued to walk on the wrong side of the tracks and is freshly out of jail.

He drinks his coffee, lingers a while, and goes to the back of the café, where the bathroom is. He locks himself inside.

---

[45] Hustlers.

Then he pulls out a piece of paper, an envelope, a pencil, and as best he can, writes a few lines in the almost illiterate hand-writing of a boy from the slums. The note is to his father; he asks for forgiveness for what he is about to do. Then he pulls out a revolver and examines it to make sure it is in working order.

He emerges from the bathroom, walks through the café, says goodbye to his friend, and walks out.

Outside, the sun is blinding. He crosses the bridge, which is almost deserted.

He crosses it slowly, as if uncertain, conflicted and yet determined.

From the bridge one can see beautiful views of the city, including small, everyday, ancient scenes: a fisherman, little boys playing on the riverbank, some girls. And the city: tran-quil rows of buildings under the sun.

Now Muchetta has left the bridge behind him. He walks across a few streets until he reaches his destination. Anony-mously, seemingly indifferently, he waits there.

He looks straight ahead; on the other side of the street lies the door of the police station. Between him and the door, while he waits, the typical, uneventful events of the afternoon go by; an old beggar picks up cigarette butts, a man emerges from his Fiat Seicento to talk to a woman who had been waiting for him, a young man walks by with a dog ... Then, all at once, a group of policemen walk out of the station, headed toward a red jeep parked in front.

Among them there is one in particular . . . his face . . . his face is tanned, and he has a mustache . . . a flashing image. Muchetta pulls out his pistol and shoots. The policeman falls to the ground, injured, near the jeep. Then Muchetta points the revolver against his temple: there he is on the ground, a corpse, a rag stretched out in the calm sunlight, among the frightened people running toward them.

II

Again, we are on the *Lungotevere*, between the Mazzini Bridge and the Vittorio Emanuele Bridge. This is a quiet, sumptuous portion of the *Lungotevere*, lined with beautiful art nouveau villas, gardens. An elderly man and woman walk together, along the gardens, under the shade of plane trees. On the other side of the river, bathed in sunlight, rises the Janiculum hill.

The conversation between the two old friends is dignified, old-fashioned, and reserved. They share few words, pervaded by a profound skepticism, almost sadness. They are two aristocrats; he is an elderly prince, from one of the oldest and most noble families in Rome.

The two take leave of each other in front of a gate; he kisses her hand, she waves. She enters her Umbertian[46] villa; he continues his walk down the *Lungotevere*. He is tired,

---

[46] In the style that became popular under Umberto I, king of Italy 1878–1900.

and the breeze blows his noble white hair across his forehead, which is moist with perspiration. He walks on, filled
with resignation, hostility. This world is no longer his. The
other beings who fill it with noise and life seem like another
species.

The tragedy occurs suddenly, at the foot of a bridge. He
is crossing the street, a trolley bus arrives at high speed, hits
him, he falls against the parapet of the bridge, people run
over . . .

The sad ritual begins: the police, the ambulance, the
mortuary.

The elderly prince is not carrying his identity papers; no
one knows who he is. In the mortuary, he is no different from
all the others.

People arrive, looking for. . . .

A poor woman comes searching for her husband. He was
unemployed, and came from their village, hidden in the
Apennines, to look for a job in Rome. He disappeared twenty
days earlier, almost a month before, without a trace. The
woman does not recognize her poor unemployed husband
in the face of the prince.

Two young brothers, factory workers, come seeking their
father, who, as they say without shame, likes to get drunk;
he disappeared from home a few days ago during one of his
binges, and no one has seen him since. They do not recognize their inebriated father in the face of the prince.

Night falls, and the somber pilgrimages come to an end.
The prince faces the first night of eternity alongside the

modest folk whom destiny has brought together in these final
moments, all unaware of each other. . . .

III

There is a celebratory atmosphere at the bar in Testaccio
where Il Trippacchio works. He's a pathetic figure in his
forties, with kids, but still a scoundrel, a kid, despite his big
belly and his almost completely bald head. All his friends and
neighbors are there in the café; they're middle aged, and yet
loud, playful, vain, and ignorant as kids. Some of them work
and some of them are unemployed, but the evenings are the
same for all of them, at the bar, at the soccer game, on the
streets, talking to their friends and taking in the evening air,
especially now that the hot summer nights are beginning.

All his friends are there: Il Budella, Il Baga, Provolone,
Pedalino, Il Capogna. They're butchers, porters, peddlers, or
they do nothing at all. They've already had a few drinks, and
they're half stewed, so they talk loudly and passionately.

The bar closes. The owner leaves. Trippacchio's friends
hang around the small, shadowy, deserted piazza. Their discussion continues, more and more animated, more and more
coarse.

Then they head home down the streets of Testaccio, their
loud, cantankerous, inebriated voices echoing against the
buildings. Trippacchio is more argumentative than usual,

and the others gang up on him. He turns mean, and everybody's blood rises.

They go for another drink at a tavern on the *Lungotevere*
that is still open; this is enough to render them completely
drunk. They come out, hollering; one of them sings, and the
others continue to argue, about nothing. But one word leads
to another, and as they start to cross the Sublicio bridge, they're
almost fighting. Trippacchio for some reason is alone against
the rest of them; the discussion heats up more and more, and
as they cross the bridge, he starts to bring up old stories, old
resentments, events from the past. They have lived near each
other for years and years, since they all went to the San Michele
school, since the war, and who knows what they've been
through together, what they know about each other, what
omertà[47] ties them to one another. Little by little, it all comes
out; the wine has loosened everyone's tongue. After they cross
the bridge, long pauses punctuated by yelling and insults, they
enter the huge old building where they live, as in a casbah.
Corridors, courtyards, stairways, all immersed in total darkness. And their insults become even more brutal.

On the landing in front of Trippacchio's door some
punches fly, and then they all jump on each other, as if they
mean to leave nothing of each other but ashes and dirty rags.
Some people emerge from their apartments. Trippacchio,

---

[47] *Omertà* is the conspiracy of silence that ties people together, as in the Mafia
or any kind of closed group.

injured and bleeding, manages to get inside his apartment, as if in flight; instead, he quickly re-emerges with a large kitchen knife in his hand.

The others hold him back and attack him with animal-like fury. Gasping, Trippacchio rolls down the stairs and comes to a stop; he does not get up. Terrified, the others run off, toward the courtyard or the attic. The stairway remains empty, unencumbered under the flickering light.

IV

A truck crosses the Testaccio bridge in the pale dawn light; it is loaded with livestock headed for the slaughterhouse.

The cattle dealer and his helpers are inside; they are athletic peasant types, servile and grim.

The boss is in the prime of life: he's around forty, strong, tall, dark-faced, with a big belly, simultaneously disfigured and strengthened by hard labor and food. He's a kind of Taras Bulba of the slaughterhouse.

Everything proceeds as usual. He is surrounded by his colleagues, other cattle dealers whom he does business with, to whom he is tied by an ancient *omertà*, all of them competing to get away with the most, and to be the biggest son of a. . . .

The animals are slaughtered, quartered, and paid for. The morning passes thus amidst blood, coarse jokes, and hard labor, all under the ferocious summer sun.

It is noon, and this Taras Bulba, along with all the other Taras Bulbas, no less powerful, large, or blood-stained, is famished; they go out to eat together. Theirs will be a Homeric banquet at a *trattoria* under a trellis across the river.

They cross the bridge, followed by their favorite laborers, the most violent and faithful of the country youths.

They reach the *trattoria* and the feasting begins.

It is as if they were eating the beasts they have just slaughtered. Their appetite reveals a hidden violence. They are the last cowboys. But they are also paradoxically quick-witted. Their jokes, allusions, and discussions are coarse but spirited.

The youths bring over some women, mostly old prostitutes, others quite young. There are four or five of them mixed in with the seven men and several youths. A group of musicians comes over as well. The other tables around them are occupied by laborers, mostly builders. The Taras Bulba of the slaughterhouse is the most violent, unbridled of all of them. Business is going well, and he is in his prime.

They eat, tell jokes, sing, and in the end, they dance. The Taras Bulba takes a spin with one of the women, a young foul-mouthed tart; then he returns to the table; in the meantime the waiter has brought over a huge piece of meat. He prepares to eat, but suddenly the world around him turns black, and he falls to the ground, struck down in a flash.

Final Episode

A few young men are sitting in a boat, one of those little row boats you see on the Tiber when you are almost in the countryside. Here we are near the Magliana, beyond the last bridge in Rome. . . .

There are three or four of them, excited by their adventure; they laugh, sing loudly, yell things at the people on the shore, exchange insults with them. They row randomly, here and there, pretending to be pirates. A group of older boys emerges from behind some bushes on the bank. They're suburban louts, dark and boisterous, with black, curly hair; a few have shaved heads.

They start to insult the kids on the boat, and then, all of a sudden, they jump into the river; in no time, they reach the boat. They're bigger, stronger, and used to having their way. One of them, who they call Sburdellino, seems to be the leader of the group; he is agile, determined, and as sharp as a knife.

They climb onto the boat. The youths try to resist, but in the end they are forced to give in. The others, led by Sburdellino, take them "hostage." They take the boat wherever they want to go; first they decide to paddle to a certain point on the riverbank to spy on a couple, but by the time they get there the couple has gone. Further down there is a group of swimmers, young kids, who are joyfully jumping into the river and swimming; they have abandoned their clothes on the grassy river bank.

Sburdellino and his friends decide to go steal their clothes. They turn the boat in that direction, excited by the roguish plan.

But suddenly Sburdellino sees something and orders the others to turn back; his friends pay no attention to him. Sburdellino protests angrily, but to no end; the others have joined forces against him, and so he jumps in the water and heads in the direction of what he had seen. Because the boat is near the bridge, the water forms whirlpools and flows on, swollen, seething, whirling.

Sburdellino is dragged away by the water, toward the pylons of the bridge. Whatever he is swimming toward looks like a rag struggling in the waters under the bridge, shimmering in the sun. Now the others look toward what is going on under the bridge and forget their mischievous enterprise.

Sburdellino is struggling violently against the whirlpool of the current that is pulling him away. The thing that looked like a rag is now visible from the boat: it is a swallow.

Will Sburdellino be able to reach it? At that particular point, the river is treacherous. The others know it, and begin to follow him in the boat.

Sburdellino is coming closer to the swallow, but the current drags them both beyond the pylons of the bridge, and they disappear. . . .

When the boat passes under the bridge, they see Sburdellino sitting on the shore, scorched by the sun, with the swallow in his hands, between his knees. His friends approach, and climb out of the boat. One of them says: "Why don't we

kill it? What'd you save it for, I wanted to see it drown."
Sburdellino, straight-faced, pays no attention to him; he is
trying to warm the swallow and dry it off. It doesn't take long
to dry, and as soon as it does, Sburdellino lets it go. It flies
away, whizzing off, chirping, and soon it is lost among the
other swallows flying above the river.

[1959]

Il Cavallo di Troia (*The Trojan Horse*), Bergamo, no. 10, Spring, 1989.

You will have noted that the episodes, which should be six, are actu-
ally five. There is no explanation for this discordance in the manuscript.
For the episode with the swallow, see the end of the first chapter of *The
Ragazzi*, and the story "La rondinella del Pacher" ("Pacher's Swallow") in
Un Paese di Temporali e di Primule (*A Place of Storms and Primroses*),
edited by Nico Naldini, Guanda, Parma, 1983, pp. 168–171.

WOMEN OF ROME

I

I see Anna Magnani sitting there, on a couch at the back of the elegant sitting room, behind a valuable antique sideboard laden with little boxes and trays of exquisite sweets. She is half hidden and says nothing. Her skin is pale, and her eyes hover like a black kerchief above her nose. She says nothing, but sits with her back straight just as her grandmother sat at her doorstep a century earlier. I can see that her silence is full of tension. Behind the black kerchief of her eyes lie still darker shadows, now interrupted, now back again, repressed like a silent belch, or released like a peal of laughter. It is clear that the people around her press in on her, and she flows into herself, like a spilled liquid returning to its vase, remaining there, quietly, on her best behavior.

She drinks the delicious champagne offered to her by her host, and she gets drunk. After a few minutes she gets up from her corner, bellows for all to hear that she is going to the bathroom, and when she returns, she sits in the center of the room, on a small chair in the middle of the green carpet. It is as if she were on a stage; she sits with her back straight and her breasts pushed forward. And they're nice breasts too, because she has just refashioned herself in the style of a hot number. And yet still she is like her grandmother; somehow her dress combines the latest fashion with the eternal fashion of the rough peasant woman. She sits defiantly.

She has removed the dark kerchief from her pale face, and her eyes float in pitch, flashing shyly and maliciously, with sidelong glances suddenly extinguished or prolonged, now with a different expression. Glances that destroy their object and make whoever looks at her feel stupid.

This feeling of being stupid in her presence immediately becomes affection. Like those lowlifes who drive up to a prostitute on a motorcycle as she waits there, absolutely still, sitting on a bench at the Baths of Caracalla. Before her air of defiance, even the coolest tough guy loses his bearings and finds himself merely standing there, as if before the statue of a miraculous saint.

From her defiant air, it is impossible to know what Anna might be hiding. But what everyone hopes is that she will

sing. An old popular song. One of those old songs that everyone knows, with some slight improvisation, a new ending
or a joke. She can only express herself by singing, because
what she has to express is something indistinct and whole:
she expresses pure life, her own, and that of generations of
Roman women who have gone before her. . . .

II

The *ragazzo* emerges from a crumbling alleyway onto the
street, itself crumbling, near the Parioletti neighborhood.
Like dried-up brooks, a series of alleys flow down from this
street in the Parioletti toward the Pigneto[48] neighborhood,
among shacks, little country houses, and new walls and buildings, cement still wet.

The *ragazzo* is dark, with dark hair; this is all that is visible in the shadows of the evening. In the dark, his white jeans
seem even whiter; they gleam like a polished mirror. He has
just put them on, and only a few creases have formed, under
the bulging pockets, at his thighs. These are the first white
jeans of the season; it is late spring, but what sweetness, heavy
with midsummer, is in the air in Torpignattara. . . .

He crosses the street, walking straight as a horse wearing
blinders, determined, fierce, ready to fight if need be in order

---

[48] Parioletti and Pigneto are two poor neighborhoods in the city.

to set things straight. There, between two Fiat Seicentos and a Morini, in the light of a late-night snack bar, two people are waiting for him.

They are two young women, terribly young, like two kittens; they are wearing summer dresses, but, because it is still cool out, they have dutifully put on little sweaters, brown, or hazelnut-colored, serious, clean. One of them is slightly taller than the other, and she has long chestnut-colored hair with an ever-so-slightly reddish tint, especially where it puffs out and curls, against the searing light of the snack bar behind her. Her little face is pale, tender; it could fit in the palm of a hand, and she has a small mouth like only pale, dark-skinned girls have: it is a bit Arab-looking, tender but not too soft, probably like that of her younger brothers, also adolescents.

The boy, with his marvelous white jeans, walks directly toward them. He says something inaudible, probably something like: "What'd you say to Maria about me, huh?" or "Say, what'd you do last night?"

She makes excuses, dutifully; she talks and talks, serious and tender. He has trouble maintaining his anger in the face of such worried, careful excuses. At first he scowls, but then flashes a relaxed, playful glance. The girl, who from the beginning sensed that his aggressive air was just a pose, slowly calms down, softens up; the threat hidden in those bright, wicked white jeans no longer frightens her.

III

He walks next to her, at a sacred pace. He stands to her left, and rests his hand on her right shoulder, holding her close. It is a protective, possessive gesture; it has lost all affectionate or even sensual connotations, and represents a kind of right of ownership. And, in order to make matters even more clear, they are walking down the Viale Trastevere, or rather crossing it, but not on the crosswalk, no, but right in the middle of traffic, between the tram turning onto the Viale from Via Induno, a 75 tram about to turn onto Viale Dandolo near the *Palazzo degli Esami*, and a row of cars is backed up all the way to the Garibaldi bridge.

But the *ragazzo*, with his rough face that looks like it has been boiled, and his hand on her shoulder holding her close, sees and hears nothing, neither the tram, nor the bus, nor the cars. Their sacred gestures and pace protect them, the two of them, the couple, from all danger. Let the tram, the buses, the cars, slow down; what we are seeing before us is youth and love, species and society, all concentrated in the two of them, in the miracle they embody.

She is possessed, protected, and symbolized; she looks as though she were in mourning. She is so serious; there is not even the shadow of a smile, present or future, on her face. She has somehow become rigid and hardened in the silent enactment of this ritual consummated by two people, on this ordinary avenue, in front of this ordinary public building, headed toward an ordinary, working-class neighborhood: she is in the center of the universe.

It is all up to them; and we must tip our hats to them. He, with his rough, flushed cheeks, looks as if he might strike anyone who is not disposed to accept such a solemn investiture, and naturally she agrees. Nuzzled, dispirited, joyless, she is on his side.

Her skin is dark, almost black, and her lips turn downward, as if she were nursing a longstanding distress; her eyes are melancholy and distracted, with a glint that suggests recent tears. Actually, there is no doubt at all; that slight glint in her eye is a tear: perhaps a tear of consolation, but still a tear. Cleverly, he cultivates this profound seriousness, adding new material to the fire: he is probably telling her that he knows people . . . He will do this, that, and the other: and she walks beside him, silently, sadly, complicitous, in his magic circle, like a novice.

IV

Everyone in Rome knows that one of the most beautiful spectacles in the city is the Porta Portese market on Sunday mornings.

I walk with a picture frame under my arm and a small inkstand in my hand through a crowd that forces me to slither like a snake between rows of stalls and blankets covered in merchandise spread out on the ground. It is Christ-

mas time, but a summer sun cooks our heads and the wobbly
chairs, dusty fabrics, false antiques, bad copies, and medals
on display. The salesmen have been there since before dawn,
and they are sleepy, under this beautiful sun; they call out,
in hoarse voices, laughing, overcome by a kind of restless-
ness just as they are every Sunday, as if they were drunk or
crazy; but one can see that they are overwhelmed with sleepi-
ness, and they could practically lie down on the spot, struck
down by exhaustion, and fall asleep between a wooden statue
of Sant'Antonio and a portrait of Il Duce.

A hysterical crowd, electrified by the sweet atmosphere
of Christmas, swarms down the road through Porta Portese,
which is about one or two miles long, beneath warehouses,
huts, and baroque ruins, and above the filthy banks of the
Tiber.

Suddenly, beyond a clump of sweaty youths, between the
curved backs of bourgeois ladies buying Christmas presents
—intimidated by this close contact with the underclasses—
and the outlines of a herd of foreigners in the midst of a
shopping spree, I catch a glimpse, like a hallucination, of a
scene from a Roman living room.

It is Mrs. Livia De S. and Mrs. Paola M. The first lady
hovers in the midst of the throng like a large swan in a muddy
pond, with a long, puffy, heraldic neck holding up a head
that is not overly large, but worthy of a great eighteenth-
century mannerist, preferably educated in Spain and de-
ceased in Sicily. Her round mouth expresses surprise, and
her eyes, placed classically halfway between nose and fore-

head, look out inexpressively and mysteriously, with a look of adolescent confusion, despite her advanced age; it is not clear whether they are blue or brown. The second lady seems shorter than her actual height (she is a real Roman, well built) because she is so fascinated by the objects laid out around her feet. Her huge eyes, rimmed in black like those of a silent screen goddess beneath a square forehead and hair as black as that of old, cameo-wearing aunts, carefully scour the merchandise that intrigues her, which her acute practical intelligence easily distinguishes from the rest.

They see me; we are like augurs, like accomplices. We compare our purchases. The two ladies are laden with copper objects. The sun burns our eyes and skin, and reflects against the objects in our hands. I think it is the first time I have met these two ladies during the daytime. But the crowd separates us, pushing us in different directions. They say goodbye, happily, shaking their copper objects and crying out: "They're for Fellini . . . for Fellini . . ." And they disappear in the sacrilegious mob.

V

Behind the Janiculum hill, up above, in the new neighborhood filled with Garibaldine mementos, the sun, at this hour, dominates in solitary splendor. The blooming wisteria, already wilted, fills the air with the fragrance of sugary sweet cadavers, and Monteverde is filled with an explosion of green, Roman green, too heavy to reveal variations or shadings, all of a piece, desperate, suffocating, and splendid.

In the sun, sitting at a small metal table of a café—without drinks—are six or seven girls: it is just the sun and them.

The little café is on the corner of Via Fratelli Bonnet and Via Carini, next to the bus stop. The passers-by can see them: the drivers of empty buses or shop assistants wandering around waiting for the workshops to open, or the attendant at the Ozo gas station which stands next to a trellis covered in greenery, like a salad. The girls are embarrassed, and so they laugh; the café owner tolerates their presence, sitting there on his metal chairs, and the few men in the vicinity glance over at them, amused by their clumsy appearance, unbrushed hair, and unfashionable clothes. They look at them as colleagues, in a comradely manner. And the girls just laugh and laugh. They are all wearing the same white smock. Even their shoes are all, practically speaking, the same shapeless, cheap, worn out shoes, worn by poor, working-class girls. It is hot out, and so they do not wear shirts or blouses under their smocks.

Their faces are marked, aged before their time. The oldest among them is not more than twenty-five years old, and yet their skin is bad, pasty, chapped. Their messy hair frames pallid, sweaty, prematurely wrinkled foreheads. Most of them are skinny, drawn. One of them, the homeliest of all, is quite small; you can tell from her protruding, taut cheekbones and from the buck teeth visible through the thin layer of flesh around her mouth, that she travels from some far-off suburb to work in the city, somewhere like Trullo, or Magliana, or Primavalle.

But she too laughs about nothing along with the others. They laugh at their senseless embarrassment, at their nurse's smocks, at their very presence, there, all together, as they attract the attention of the men around them, at the drudgery of their lives. They laugh without subtlety, and without even a hint of brutality. They are there, whoever wants them can come and get them; poor factory workers, homely and marked by hard labor, but, even so, as good as any other when it comes to certain things. . . .

VI

How little my mother[49] is, tiny as a schoolgirl, diligent, frightened, but determined to do her duty to the end. These women frighten her; she watches them with apprehension. They are her age, or even younger, much younger in some cases. But she is sweet and delicate, and has remained a young girl compared to them; they are adults. Each one of them seems to conceal a man inside of her. Less so when they are young, or at least it is less apparent (but what to make of

---

[49] Pasolini's mother, Susanna Colussi, was from Friuli, in the north of Italy.

their overt meanness, their rage, the rancor one sees in their eyes?). But as time goes by, the man they carry inside grows and comes to the surface: his voice, and over time even his face, his protruding chin, his pouting lower lip, his enlarged nostrils, his hairiness. They are frightening as they stand at their vegetable stands; my mother is right to tremble slightly as she asks for an artichoke or cherries in her light, mild, ancient, Veneto accent. The women grab and pack up the artichokes with coarse rage. They have other things on their mind. But when you think about it, it's hard to imagine what these other things could be. After all, they are fruit vendors: strong as mules, hard as stone, ill humored, and suffering from heart problems. But fruit vendors. Their lives are limited to two or three things: a small, dark house, old as the Colosseum, in a dark alley behind the Campo dei Fiori, or perhaps in a new neighborhood like the Ina-Casa, San Paolo, or Via Portuense; two, three or four children, half boys and half girls, half toddlers and half adolescents, perhaps one of them in the army; and a husband with a beat-up car, who speaks as if he had a boiling hot battery in his throat, red in the face and pasty skinned, with a face so wide you could fit all of Terracina in it. The usual. So why the attitude? Why do they act as if they were the cupolas of Saint Peter's? Because they are like cows or pigs, truly ancient, pure, and vital; they were born before Christ, and their philosophy is that of the Stoics, as interpreted by the people. Life is a battle; there's no mystery about it. We are doomed to suffer, but survive, and get on with it, but with rage. Maybe there's a Christian, Catholic God, who must be placated with candles and prayer; and then we get on with it. It's here, in this life, that we are rewarded or punished: food and drink are the reward, and delinquent kids or a drunk husband are the punishment. Men are weak, traitorous, lazy, lewd; it's up to the women to keep life on track no matter how it is handed down to us when we're born. And the painful, maddening certainty in those warty, pimply faces frightens us, weak, uncertain Christians that we are. . . .

VII

The Vicolo del Cinque at dusk: a dingy alley, cobbled with stones and old bricks, settles down for the night, the sun blazing through in patches on the rooftops. People have finished working for the day. The *ragazzi* and kids are dressed up—not quite in party dress, but in their clothes for the evening, which is a sort of party. They loiter on the sidewalk next to the freshly closed shutters of the shops, in front of barber shops, at pinball machines, on motorcycles. The little ones are dirty because all day they've been playing in the dust, and they go on playing, serene and unworried. The old folks, in the long dusk of life, take walks, and they too are dirty because what's the point of cleaning up and fixing one's hair at that age? They are no longer full of mischief, but their

eyes, mean and turbid, reveal that at heart they are still piti-
fully adolescent. . . . The alley is dominated by those who are
absent: young men and their older companions who are out
drinking, under the same sun, surrounded by the same smells
and sounds, further along the Tiber or toward the end of the
Via della Lungaretta, or under the brush-woods of the Janiculum hill. . . . Life in the alley goes on without them; one
day they will return, clean-shaved like supplicants. Meanwhile, the others, those who are present, the beardless youths
and the old cronies stinking of wine, continue on, chewing
American gum or cursing to themselves, hoping to one day
join the ranks of the absent, hoping that nothing will change.
This life is guarded and watched over by those who seem
almost not to exist at all: crowding in doorways, standing
framed in the windows, some with the same dark skin and
licorice eyes as their sons, others with the softness of a
younger brother, and still others with the animal rage of their
fathers. They are like an audience, or a backdrop, anonymous
and uniform, spread throughout the alleyway, mixing with
the men as oil mixes with vinegar. The men act, move, laugh;
they watch, wait, grumble. And yet they are the conscience
of life in the alleyway, of life as it is, not as it should be. People
who have lost hope do not hope for their lives to improve;
people who are condemned to darkness do not desire the
light. Only a very young girl here and there, whose breasts
have swelled under her sweater in the past two years, begins
to rebel against this ancient confinement, this servitude to

men for whom the only recognizable code of honor is the subjection of women. There she is, moving about in her pretty dress, crying out. . . .

Donne di Roma (*Women of Rome*), introduction by Alberto Moravia, seven stories by Pier Paolo Pasolini and 104 photographs by S. Waagenaar, Il Saggiatore, Milan, 1960.

(RI)COTTA CHEESE[50]

I

An *art nouveau* sitting room. We see a group of relatives standing in two rows, the shorter ones in front and the taller ones behind. They are all ugly. And then they begin to dance the twist (it is 1963),

> *Come color che un colpo al basso ventre*
> *Piega in avanti col sedere indietro,*
> *E furba beatitudine negli occhi.*

---

[50] This is the title of a short film Pasolini made in 1962, with Orson Welles, Laura Betti, and Mario Cipriani.

As laid low by a kick,
He leans forward, rear protruding,
With sly simplicity in his eyes. . . .

They vociferate and exclaim, in the accent of Adalgisa,[51] while the Marquise Crespina Agnellini in Pirelloni sings in Milanese. The words "Viva il nostro Papà" ("Long live Papa!") ring out in the soundtrack, like a litany.

II

Five or six extreme close-ups of Prince De Curtis,[52] "Papà," whose exclamations over the phone reveal the following information to even the most inattentive viewer:

a) He is an important Milanese industrialist.
b) He is about to launch a new product, and aims to win over millions of his fellow Italians.
c) Meanwhile, he is closing a deal (speculative real estate, selling off an entire street of eighteenth- and nineteenth-century buildings) worth billions of *lire*.
d) He is following the local elections in a city in the "heel of the boot,"[53] where he intends to build a branch of his business; he is seeking a "straw man" among the local lawyers.

---

[51] The main character of Gadda's novel of the same name.
[52] Antonio De Curtis, known as Totò, was a famous and beloved Neapolitan comedian who appeared in dozens of films. He also acted in several of Pasolini's films.
[53] Puglia.

e) He is also the president of a large film production company, which is producing a film called *Beat the Bourgeoisie* to be released shortly in Italy. He is worried about the political and religious undertones of the film, and has decided to

f) Attend a poetry reading by the film's screenwriter at the Bagnacaudi Bookstore (in order to appear in the publicity photographs), but simultaneously to

g) Invite a group of youths from the Italo-Hysterical Committee (the activist appendage of the P.I.S.S. party) to the sacred event so that they will cover the poet with insults and ignominy, and finally, to

h) Find a lawyer who will file a complaint against the poet. There must be some defamatory crime that a damned poet can be accused of!

III

Contro la cornea il twist *del* boom.
Adesso nel ballo dei subnormali ipersviluppati
Si sentiranno lacerti di osanna al Capitalismo all'antica,
Altro che Neo-Capitalismo e Centro-Sinistra,
Altro che Giovanni XXIII e Giovanni XXIII,
Viva la "Edison," porca miseria!

Watch it go, the twist and boom,
The dance of the hyperdeveloped simpletons,

Fragments of Hosannas to old-style Capital,
Forget Neo-Capitalism and the Center-Left,
Forget John XXIII
Long live Edison, hot diggity damn!

IV

The Bagnacaudi bookstore. Daytime, interior shot. The poet is reading political verses before an audience of intellectuals, including Prince De Curtis, who from now on I will call Mater Dollarosa.[54]

Screams, blows, and hooting can be heard from outside the bookstore.

The noise increases, people emerge. Scuffles. The police intervene.

Bagnacaudi bookstore. Daytime, exterior shot. We see the youths of the Italo-Hysterical Committee in a long shot: ugly, fat, spineless, lazy, stupid, and with signs that read: "Long live Papà," "Long live the Motherland," "Long live Morality," "Long live words that start with capital letters," etc.

Chaos, blows, indignation.

Mater Dollarosa watches all of this with the mysteriously aloof air of the master.

---

[54] In the original, his name is *"Mater Danarosa,"* twisting *"Mater Dolorosa"* to mean "Mother Moneybags."

His mystery and aloofness become concrete, as he moves away toward the margins of the increasing chaos, toward the small trees of the Via della Dolce Vita, and there. . . .

. . . A little girl appears, a little girl with eyes like freshly baked bread, like a sea full of fish, blue as an overflowing sky, so pure that their gaze strikes in the middle of the chest like a blow, silent, wide open, severe, candid. (The child is a beggar who plays the violin, using Chaplin's strategy.)

Mater Dollarosa asks her questions, and she responds, diligently, shyly: first name, family name . . . she responds in an innocent voice, filled with joy, a voice from beyond history. . . . Her father's name was Stracci[55] and he died on the cross. . . . Yes, he died on the cross while he was playing the role of the good thief in a film. . . . He died of hunger, or of indigestion, because he had eaten too much . . . RICOTTA . . . She laughs and cries as she says it. . . . Then she begins to play her little tune on the violin, with her ancient, deaf grandmother at her side. . . . Slowly, the tune becomes a sublime melody by Bach, and close-ups of the Mater Dollarosa and the young girl alternate over and over.

V

We are in a neighborhood not far from downtown Rome, in fact very near Saint Peter's basilica. The dome of the ba-

---

[55] Rags.

silica is always there, visible beyond gardens, dusty vacant lots, disorderly clumps of shacks, piles of garbage, alleys, ragged thickets. And beyond, we can see newly built tall buildings, the product of new wealth, glimmering in the sunlight.

Mater Dollarosa climbs out of the car (long backwards pan) and walks into this mess. He appears pale in the sun.

He is looking for the little Stracci girl.

He hands a fistful of change to each person he speaks to, inquiring after the little girl. He follows the classic technique (a ballet if you will, a bit Zavattinian[56] in style; the poor fools take the bills, which fly off like crows from the sun-battered neighborhood).

In the end he traces the Stracci girl back to her dismal shack; it is smelly and shriveled as a dried cod. Mater Dollarosa wants to hear her play the violin. Again, we see close-ups of Mater Dollarosa and the little girl alternating over and over again; they are reduced to traces of tenderness by the celestial sound of Bach.

VI

The twist tune (circa 1963) returns. It is a twist tune for vipers who dance.

---

[56] Cesare Zavattini was a scriptwriter of Neorealist films like *Shoeshine* and *Bicycle Thieves*.

Come color che un po di pepe al culo
Fa rotear sul perno della pancia
Ritratti, come vermini acciaccati

Like people, who with pepper in their ass,
Roll about squirming on their belly,
And turn away, like vermin struck down.

It is the pain caused by the loss of the certainty of capital in the face of existential uncertainty.

VII

But Mater Dollarosa is no longer capitalist; now, he is neo-capitalist, for quasi-mystical reasons of "internal historicity"— there is no other reason, except a punch in the face —and the Pietas and Amore of classical times have been transformed into Action. But more on that later. For now, Dollarosa is making plans to replace the shacks with modern villettes, a supermarket, a day care center, and other similar things.

The former shack dwellers are happy, and they send post cards to their relatives in Sardegna and Calabria, inviting them to come and visit. (Gags in Zavattini or Sonego[57] style).

The hypo-historical love of the Mater Dollarosa for the little Stracci girl [who will be the angel in a film about the

---

57 Rodolfo Sonego: a screenwriter of Italian comedies.

Gospel—PPP] is at its point of culmination, still accompanied by the sacred music of anthropologically human times. So much so that Stracci's brothers, who from the tenderest age have gone to the Paraguletti School, decide to blackmail him . . . And, under the stockfish sun of the world of the hungry, the money flows. . . .

VIII

The Marquise Crespina Agnellini in Pirelloni and all of her relatives put on their war paint, stick a feather in their hair, and pick up their war axes. The melody of the twist tune is now an arrangement from *Rigoletto*, and the students of the Jesuits and Sorelle Dorotee dance, as they hurl savage insults against their ex-Papà:

LOCO LOCO LOCO LOCO!

CRAZY CRAZY CRAZY CRAZY!

Fade-out.

IX

At this point we witness the sacred silence of the court. The beautiful art-nouveau sitting room, which decades later will be turned into a Turkish Bath, represents Dannunzian majesty in all its tragic ugliness.

Then we will see, in a long shot, taken with the maximum respect, the entrance of the judges, etc.

Suddenly, in the respectful silence, there will be a close-up of the director of *Beat the Bourgeoisie*, who covets the little Stracci girl (in the witness box).

He is struck by an idea: he wants to discover her, launch her, turn her into a Diva! He calls the photographer, a big paparazzo among the little paparazzi, and *flash, flash, flash*, the little Stracci girl is immortalized, with the Crucifixes and Judges' gowns as a backdrop, flashing her smile. Her smile makes one think of far-off Arab lands, blue sugar.

Then, turning the movie-camera to 12 frames per second, employing epic Chaplinesque acceleration—I will show the parade of witnesses. They will file past at high speed: the Relatives, vomiting out attacks and horrendous accusations of FOLLY toward their ex-Papà. He sits with his double chin like Christ on the dock. After testifying, each witness gives concrete form to his moral accusation by picking up a RICOTTA pie from a tray held up by an old family servant, and hurling it at the face of his father, uncle, brother, cousin, brother-in-law, father-in-law, son-in-law, respectively: "Take that, you crazy bastard, take this ricotta in your face, and get out of here, go to hell, crazy bastard, crazy, bastard, crazy . . . !"

Dissolve.

Now it is the poet's turn to testify. The movie camera returns to normal speed, and in the peaceful light that filters in from the sweet world outside the vanilla-colored windows, he explains the reasons for the Lombard Capitalist's descent to folly, along the road of neo-capitalism, and to a place outside of rational thinking. This descent has been brought on by the ancient emotion that is Love, destined to decline quickly in the real world of neo-capitalism where feelings will have to become decidedly false in order to mask brutal reality.

Dissolve.

The cry of a predatory bird announces the return of the Court. And, with the maximum respect to the National-Bathhouse architecture, the Court pronounces its verdict: EXILE.

X

There is a poster on the streets (the same streets Archie walked down in America in the 1930s). It features Mater Dollarosa's double chin. Honest, mortified, and silent, he looks out with his exile eyes, while, underneath, the viper's words glint in the darkness: "Catholics, do not vote for Mater

Dollarosa: he will betray you with the social-communists."
(Any reference to such a poster, similar to those which were
put up last year by the MSI[58] in protest against Fanfani and
Moro,[59] is purely coincidental.)

The real living Mater walks by his effigy. Without his
luxury car, dragging his feet, accompanied by Saint Francis's
horse, he seems rather out of sorts. Standing before a school
building, the fat, ugly, stupid mama's boys hold up their signs
as they watch him, with the irony of the brave and pure. Despite being exquisite exemplars of the bourgeoisie, they in-
dulge in the warmongering, lowly violence of the mob. And
the "spectaculum vulgi" walks on, with his double chin, followed by a chorus of farts, down Hobo Street.

XI

Hobo Street leads to the humanistic world of Love. The
dirty-and-dusty neighborhood dominated by a gold-and-
marble dome. Mater Dollarosa goes from hovel to hovel,
searching for the little Stracci girl, the angel with eyes like
freshly baked bread who is the emblem of that Love. But
he no longer has money with which to buy information;

---

[58] The MSI (Movimento Sociale Italiano) was the neo-Fascist party.
[59] Amintore Fanfani and Aldo Moro were both Prime Ministers from the Christian Democratic Party.

he must beg for it instead. (It is a Zavattinian ballet in reverse, where those who have already benefited, who clearly reveal their newfound sense of self-sufficiency, contempt, and boredom toward their ex-benefactors, turn away from them with a dry, quick, explicit turn like the characters in Capra's films. The noble savage is not so noble. And why should he be?)

The Mater reaches the Stracci's hovel, but the little girl isn't home. She has gone over to the shimmering sky of the Gaioni, the Sandrellis, the Spaaks.[60] Left behind is a group of male relatives from Sardegna and Calabria, still dark and threatening, lost as wolves in their alloglossia.

XII

Twist di trinfo dei Parenti tutti
Con osanna osanna al Corriere della Sera,
E appelli alle ombre di Balbo e di Schuster.

Triumphant twist for all the relatives
Hosanna, hosanna, to the *Corriere* della Sera,[61]
They call out to the shadows of Balbo and Schuster.[62]

---

[60] Cristina Gaioni, Stefania Sandrelli, and Agnès Spaak were all famous movie stars of the time.

[61] A conservative daily newspaper.

[62] Italo Balbo and Ildefonso Schuster: Balbo was the Fascist governor of Libya at the same time that Schuster was the Cardinal of Milan.

XIII

Mater Dollarosa is now a hobo, and like a good hobo, he wanders through the mud and dust of the slums, along the burning knife's-edge of the far-off high rises. He is sinister, horrible, in his tattered overcoat, battered shoes, and ragged beard. With his greatcoat, his shoes worn to nothing, and his three-day beard.

I'm huuuuuuungry goddamnit. Goddamnit, what is there to eat? He mumbles as he walks under an escarpment filled with bedpan handles, medicine bottles, cotton wool stained with iodine, rotten basket bottoms, and dead cats with bared teeth. . . . Finally, he finds a trash can and looks inside for something to eat. A dog approaches him, with the same intentions. But out of courtesy, the dog pretends to be there by chance; he stretches out and licks his chops distractedly. But the Mater moves to one side, and the two dig through the trash together like good friends. They dig around, and every so often they find something to eat; meanwhile, they begin to converse. Mater feels that he is close to the end, and he would like to say his last words to his one, courteous, casual friend. But he has no "last words," only the desire to speak them . . . He tries and tries, but finds no words to express his desires, as a capitalist or as a hobo. He doesn't know anything; he doesn't know what's happened to him, or what has happened or will happen to the world, or the causes of injustice, pain, love, or the absence of love. It's all there somewhere, but he cannot reach it. And so he dies, without leaving behind even a single word.

The dog, poor saint, mumbles a prayer (or if this seems like an insult to religion, a funereal elegy), and then trots off, climbing up the grass that lies on the escarpment in clumps like scabies.

L'Unità, Rome, December 6, 1964. Subsequently in *Linea d'ombra*, Milan, No. 4, February 1984.

PART II

CHRONICLES OF ROME

THE DISAPPEARING WILD GAME OF THE ROMAN COUNTRYSIDE

The twenty-three thousand hunters of Rome are worried. For example, they are no longer permitted to take their auxiliaries (read: dogs) with them on the tram, except at certain times of day. Therefore, if a hunter lives in the Monte Mario or Parioli neighborhoods, when he returns, dead tired and loaded with game from the fields of Cesano or Palestrina, he must walk an additional four or five miles with his faithful auxiliary. In addition, the reporting of a stolen hunting dog is such a bureaucratic process that it is pointless to even bother going to the commissary of Pincopallino ... But I digress. The principal, constant cause for worry is always the same: it is the wildlife itself.

Does the hunter love or hate the hare? Clearly, his aim is to kill it. But to hear him talk, his voice emanating such affectionate, protective, intimate, passionate inflections, one would think that he was talking about his lover rather than his victim. Today, the Roman hunter is downtrodden because wild game in the region is disappearing, *dying*. And, the great irony is that no subject could be closer to the hunter's heart than the survival of these animals. More and more, the hares, woodcocks, pheasants, and partridges of the Roman countryside are worryingly absent from their Sunday *rendezvous* with their deadly admirers.

It is useless to even speak of migratory wildlife. Land reclamation, agricultural development, deforestation, and the advance of populated areas have destroyed all but the legend of such animals. So all efforts are dedicated to the conservation of non-migratory wildlife, the main preoccupation of our twenty-three thousand hunters.

As we all know, unity is strength, and so a provincial association of hunters has come into existence in Rome. It is thriving; inscription is obligatory, and all hunters believe that this is a good thing. Roman hunters have decided to form a large family, and the city is littered with constellations and networks of hunters' sub-committees and associations. From the Garbatella neighborhood to Trastevere and on to Prati, there is no alley where this passion does not nest. Once a year, the great family of hunters comes together and publicizes its list of concerns, topped yearly by two eternal dilemmas: the disappearance of wild game, and the burning issue of wildlife preserves.

This year the aficionados came together at the Cola Di Rienzo theater, carrying the issue of *Stadio Sport* magazine dedicated to them in their jacket pockets. It goes without saying that one does not *become* a hunter, but rather is born one; one is born with all the somatic and psychic characteristics required to be a hunter. And when I say that a "family" came together at the Cola di Rienzo theater, I am not using peremptory rhetoric, but stating an evident fact: these are brothers in the hunt, their passion binds them together. If there is such a thing as the "lazy Roman," one who displays a sumptuous Bellian idleness, there exists also the cautiously hard working Roman. Hunters belong to this last category; they are tram drivers, shop owners, postal workers. They have the friendly look of the *paterfamilias*, still young at heart, like so many overweight Aldo Fabrizis.[63]

In the Cola Di Rienzo theater, dressed in their finest, they determinedly confront their most serious problems.

Problem number one: repopulation. This was the subject of a yearly speech by the president of the hunting association, Commendatore Pistolesi. In 1948, 92 hares, 108 partridges, and 10 pheasants were released in areas undergoing repopulation. In 1949, the numbers were 330 hares, 483 partridges, and 214 pheasants, at a cost of 6 million *lire*!

It must be noted that Italian breeders are not very productive, so that more than half of the hares, partridges, and

---

[63] A comic Italian actor of rather wide girth.

pheasants come from Bohemia. These imports contribute to the strengthening of our own local species.

The disappearance of wild game is due also, as always, to the work of predators. The Association is waging a battle against these predators to the last drop of blood, in the form of thousand-*lire* notes (to the order of one million two hundred thousand *lire*). And the results, in the 1949 hunting season, were highly satisfactory: as evidence of this, the association was sent the craniums of two wolves, 1303 foxes, 907 wildcats, martens, polecats, and weasels, etc. So, that million plus I mentioned was spent for prizes to the killers of predators and for the purchase of strychnine snacks. So far in the current year, 1950, 475 foxes have been killed, an unprecedented figure in the history of the section designated to Rome.

And then there is the Fifth Column: poachers.

At the mention of poachers, resentful, vibrant, and fervent exclamations of protest were heard. But this is pure cynicism, a national protest against a national vice. It is a known fact that Italians are thieves. Predators have cost the group almost a million and a half *lire*, but the poachers have cost them seven million. An entire legion, made up of *carabinieri*,[64] gamekeepers, and park rangers, has been mobilized against them. Hundreds of thousands of *lire* were awarded to the issuers of fines against poachers. And the plague of poaching, ravager of game, is still endemic in the Roman

---

[64] Military police.

countryside. More money is needed. More involvement is needed from the Ministry of Agriculture and Forestry.

And now it is time to discuss the second most important problem facing Rome's twenty-three thousand hunters: hunting preserves. The group's greatest enemy, after the Fifth Column.

It is a burning issue. The President of the association treats it with a definite, and perhaps excessive (such is the opinion of some especially sanguine hunters) delicacy. The twelve large hunting preserves in the province do not fulfill the requirements of the law, and are constantly found to be inadequate; in addition, they are harmful to the areas that surround them. For this reason, the movement against hunting preserves in Rome and its outlying areas is extremely strong. The preserves should be brought up to standard or should be abolished. The issue was aggressively addressed, with more countrified and focused oratory verve, by an elderly hunter who was generally and sympathetically cheered on. Without hesitating, he brought up the scandal of the Lunghezza and Lunghezzina preserves, whose licenses had been revoked and then renewed by the provincial hunting authorities. Duke Grazioli's pledges to improve the standards of the hunting preserves under his management turned out to be sailor's promises; the preserve continued to be a purely speculative enterprise. The technicians who had gone to monitor the area in order to revoke the order were bamboozled; the Duke and his lawyer Stacchina (the hunters' true enemy), had arranged for thirty mangy pheasants to be set free the day before the monitors' arrival. Now these hunting preserves, and particularly those of Lunghezza and Lunghezzina, are a disgrace to the hunter; first, because they attract migratory game, which naturally prefers to take refuge amidst the abundant forests of the preserves rather than in the meager countryside that surrounds them; and second, because they also concentrate the non-migratory game, attracting it away from the surrounding free zones. "Hares and pheasants aren't stupid!" shouts the old hunter among the approving chuckles of the assembly. In conclusion, in order to at least partially remedy these inconveniences, the concessionaries should be forced to breed and set free non-migratory game, which they never do (except for Dr. Stacchina's thirty mangy pheasants). In addition, due to the expansion of the city, the Lunghezza and Lunghezzina preserves today lie just outside Rome, and in the opinion of the group such areas should be made available to the less-than-well-off hunter "with his ripped shirt and old harquebus." Of course, one could turn the Villa Borghese[65] into a hunting preserve, for the benefit of the affluent hunter. . . .

Il Quotidiano, Rome, August 9, 1950.

---

[65] The Villa Borghese is an urban park that lies in an elegant part of town, near the Via Veneto.

THE END OF A POST-WAR ERA

The setting is a pizzeria, with the rural night of Rome condensing all around. A group of young people order some wine, and the waiter makes it his business to allow the requisite quarter of an hour to pass before serving them. Small groups of people, totally disparate and yet identical, sit around white, dirty tables. On one side sits a small family with a little girl who is immersed in a long conversation with her glass, enormous in her hands. In another corner sit four intensely anonymous friends. And over there sits a couple; he is in blue, she is wearing heavy make-up, and they are from the North. In the infernal, sterilized hole lined in white tiles, the cook curls up like one of the cats around the Pantheon. Two musicians, a guitarist and an accordionist, enter and begin to play, rigid as officiating priests or traffic cops.

They play the tune from the Third Man and *"Che mele,"*[66] creating a small world, isolated from the Holy Year, the amusement park outside, and the neighborhood youths on their evening stroll, lazy and nocturnal, along the *Lungotevere.*

Who could ever suspect that these young people I mentioned before, who have ordered their wine, so slow to arrive, are probably the Matisse, Cecchi, or De Chirico of the future? Or even the friends of a future Matisse? There is no hint of the *Giubbe Rosse*[67] or of the Parisian café about this desperate pizzeria, and you won't overhear any talk of art, or of any other topic for that matter, except the miseries of life. Then, when the conversation warms up with the wine, which has finally arrived, perhaps we will hear a slightly more tender and expansive inflection of the voice. But what is the subject of their conversation? The painter's Piedmontese grandmother, the writer's Emilian grandmother? So measured, miraculously light, modest, and discreet. A piece from the arts page, circa 1950: the grandmother, consumed by *petit bourgeois* or peasant misery, but saved by an equilibrium which is now a thing of the past. . . .

It is the twilight of a post-War era. The sun has set on the far-off chapters of beautiful prose. And enthusiasm is in its last throes. A faceless skepticism is cutting away the youthful, external, and spectacular appendices of internal monologue: a river which has disappeared in the Karstic landscape

[66] A popular song from 1949, filled with sexual innuendo. It goes: "Oh the apples, the apples, I'll show you . . ."
[67] A famous literary café in Florence.

of a climate suitable for an even more clandestine and apolitical version of Giuseppe Belli. Meanwhile, those who are not Belli go to pizzerias searching unsuccessfully for a spark of *Sturm und Drang*, overwhelmed by this most Kafkan of centuries.

Meanwhile, the future famous critic (who will have no youthful memories), speaks, carried away by unliterary discourse, about the explosion of a powder keg. "Our captain," he says, "was only a few hundred yards away when it happened and he ran over. As he helped carry away the dead bodies, and the scraps and pulp of dead bodies, he found one whose bones had been pulverized by the shock wave of the blast. The muscles had melted away and the body had shrunk into a swollen, rounded dwarf, about four feet tall. Our captain wrapped it in a piece of canvas, tying the ends." Our future Matisse's twenties are filled with talk of these subjects.

Once the ways of the post-War era have disappeared, we will have to reconsider them seriously, clinically. It is the crime pages of the newspaper (not the culture page) that matter to these young *litterati*; that is where they find tales of life in this world that is condemned to death.

The Emilian poet hopes that the atomic bomb will be dropped soon, so that everything can begin anew: humanity is saturated, filled to the limit with both masterpieces and trash. When a crisis has become as complex, stratified, and chronic as this one, the only remedy is to depersonalize it, to become another, to begin again. Some people do it: why shouldn't the world? The atomic bomb could force it to do so.

Meanwhile, the crime pages are bursting with news: the *litterati* walk in the shoes of the suicide victims, feel the *splat!* of the body as it falls against the sidewalk from the third floor. They experience the last half hour of the unemployed man before he takes his life; they jump into the Tiber, full of bodies, flowing amid scoffingly rational architecture. But they say these things as if they were giving a report, in the hoarse voice that comes after emotion. They keep the real body of their anguish to themselves, perhaps for a time when they shall cross the Piazza Navona in silence, or walk down the *Lungotevere*. So much daily realism has immunized them to the realism of the American, Sartrian novel; it has been demystified as a genre. The lovely, florid prose of the twenties and forties has been left behind, with regret. Now the *litterati* who see themselves authentically as such introduce the stories of the crime pages into their interior monologue, dipped in their own anxieties, in the sewer of 1950.

Here is another crime story, dished up by the Piedmontese painter: "Bologna, or thereabouts. A thief is creeping out of a courtyard with two rabbits stuffed in his shirt, but he is not quick enough, and another thief, with the same intentions, catches him in the act. The second thief's dilemma is this: If I don't sound the alarm, and my colleague is found out, I will be considered his accomplice. So it is better if I sound the alarm. And so he begins to yell, and throws himself on the fugitive. The owner of the rabbits comes out, armed, and shoots them both. The two are brothers." The story is Bandellian:[68] But what about the setting? What about the brothers' temperate weekends in the neighborhood, an infernal suburb, their spirits constantly subjugated by the ticking of the gas meter?

These are the "brothers" of the members of this latest generation of *litterati*, dismally ambitious, renunciatory, obsessed. They do not have nocturnal, quarrelsome friendships, but relationships based on "taste," the deadly common denominator, based on a sympathy which is understood rather than communicated. These are relationships based on an epidemic which has infected them and rendered them identifiable as part of a sect. Relationships based on modesty, failure . . . in the best of cases. They cannot be accused of living "outside of reality," as in the case of other *litterati*; this is a literary generation made up of captives of the crime pages. Faced with their "equals," they feel that it is meaningless to represent them; rather, they must embody them. So much for documentation! Crime stories require dark realism. But on the page? Should our friends embody their subjects to the point of creating shocking objects to be flung in the faces of those who possess an imagination inversely proportional to their wealth? Or should they renounce even this last possibility of escape—real, concrete escape—and remain inside their subjects, in the presence of the amorphous sewer? The young literary types do not know how to resolve this conundrum; these are useless questions, and the world

---

[68] Alfredo Bandelli, author of songs of social protest.

does not ask them. The world is busy with its grim business of shady dealings, which does not bother with literary types. Business dealings take place all around them, a vertiginous syndrome. Look closer and you will find a kind of prostitution strangely like suicide.

It is not that people today are wicked or stupid; they are simply deaf. The thundering of the machine they have set in motion and which carries them toward the precipice is so loud that the far-off cries of those who have been excluded by the machine *because they hold no ticket* never reach the deafened ears of that joyous assemblage.

La libertà d'Italia, Rome, October 6, 1950.

ROME AND GIUSEPPE BELLI

My most recent discovery is Belli, and it is certainly one of my greatest, given that it has coincided with my discovery of Rome. It is a discovery I share, not without pride, by analogy (and perhaps due to certain affinities, even if I do not possess a hundredth of his natural abilities) with the portentous Gadda. I identify Belli's poetry, like Rome, with a certain mixture of facility and violence: In it, he decants the manner of speaking of common people, who express themselves within certain patterns of linguistic forms (which they would never violate, even in their most joyful moments, at the cost of their honor) into a new form of linguistic invention. This invention consists of Belli's selective treatment of reality, in the dramatic duration, in the style of Caravaggio, of his fourteen hendecasyllabic lines. If someone today attempted to imitate his manner, he would be performing a work of literary criticism rather than one of poetry. Between the common man of 1833–34 and today's common man lies the entire history of Italy, comprising a radical change in his way of life. It is true that in Rome it is still more accurate to speak of "plebeian folk" (the aristocratic plebe of the Trastevere, of the suburbs, etc.) than of a proletariat, and that many linguistic particularities have remained intact (for example the terms of obscene language within the confines of that conservative linguistic island that is sexual life, which in Rome is anything but secret). Even so, an evolution has taken place. The Bellian types who operate today in Rome (except for people like Mario Dell'Arco, who in attempting to distance themselves from Belli return to him through their gusto for words cut off from their meaning) are practically tone deaf. Belli could hear an infinity of new allocutions among his inhabitants of Trastevere and Borgo Pio, including those who had been forced by the Fascist demolitions to emigrate to the suburbs of Primavalle, Quarticciolo, Tiburtino, and Pietralata, where they formed new linguistic and moral areas, slightly beyond the inflamed modernity of Trastevere and Borgo, and mixed in with the oafs just arrived from Cassino, Puglia, Emilia Romagna, and Sardinia. Given the subversive, exhibitionistic, open nature of the Roman "man of the people," toughened in his joy, he conforms with a conscientiousness not found in speakers from any other city to the types found in the "*commedia romana*":[69] the *dritto*, the *malandro*, the *fijo de na mignotta*, the *greve*, etc.[70] Belli must have lifted many of his verses directly from reality, but without violence, referring back to the direct, real interests of his hoarse and slightly liquored up speaker. His skepticism derived from a common, sensual tension. Belli offers no theories; on the other hand, it is easy to perceive the lack of realism of the hendecasyllabic verse reproduced by Cesare Pascarella from the account of the patriot Mancini[71] (in Il Gandolin's[72] *Gli uomini che ho conosciuto*[73] he writes: the enemy was so close that *"quasi je potemio sputà in faccia."*[74]). These are unreal, dangerously rhetorical words, in part because Pascarella's speaker no longer fits into the "common" forms, attracted by a *petit bourgeois* temptation, but most of all because Pascarella has violated, beforehand, the "common speech" which he employed according to the teachings of Belli, by rendering it absurdly high-minded and nationalistic. He preserved its "common" qualities only in order to provide a superficial crust of color, revealing the errors of a quite unimaginative lack of historical perspective.

---

[69] Literally, "Roman Comedy," a reference to the characters of the *Commedia dell'Arte*, translated to the Roman context.

[70] The sly fox, the crook, the bastard (*mignotta* means whore in Roman dialect), and the lout.

[71] Pasquale Stanislao Mancini, a leader of the *Risorgimento*.

[72] Pen name of Luigi Arnaldo Vassallo, a famous nineteenth-century journalist.

[73] *The Men I've Known*, a collection of the writings of Vassallo.

[74] In Roman dialect: "we could almost spit in his face." The line has 11 syllables, like the hendecasyllabic period of Dante's verses.

The truth is that Pascarella did not have a good ear for the speech of his time, early twentieth-century Italy. He started off with Bellian notions (an ahistorical Belli, frozen in time, who had not evolved along with his people) and achieved an epic form of *petit bourgeois* tastes, drastically reducing the infinite variations of speech of the common folk, which can only be free if it is completely real. The "patriotic" function of the inhabitant of the Trastevere in Pascarella is an extremely dangerous limitation. If we wanted to bring the Bellian "method" (giving total freedom to the speaker) into the present, what results would we obtain? Contemporary Bellians (if they exist, after the mistreatments of Pascarella and Trilussa—only Zanazzo, a good, minor example, is in the Bellian tradition) are pure academics; they do not realize that "social" consciousness has *also* reached the Roman masses, providing their satire with new subjects and tonalities. They do not see the potential for poetry in this fact, blinded perhaps by the contrast between the nascent proletariat among these masses and the ancient, poetic "common folk." They do not see that corruption, vice, delinquency, are much more generalized today, especially in the outlying neighborhoods; in the Trastevere, crime has a certain classical, aristocratic quality. Or that the jargon has changed, acquiring an infinity of new turns of phrase, expressions, and allusions. It has discovered new outlets for emotion and lexical techniques for wheedling and cajoling, for expressing an existence which is conducted on the knife's edge of the most extreme modernity (best manifested by *dritteria*[75]), lying somewhere between the Sunday afternoon stabbing and the Regina Coeli prison.

The weakening influence of Catholicism and the papacy on the Roman masses—now, in the outlying neighborhoods, which are completely unbelieving, the level of superstition is much slighter than in the Rome of the past—has perhaps caused the baroque archetype of the joyful Roman populace (with its dark background, its Caravaggesque chiaroscuri) to fade, and replaced them with an atmosphere that one could call "picaresque," especially after the recent German and Anglo-Saxon occupations. The language has a drier, more novelesque air. Here are a few verses by some of the most modern of speakers: I was riding my bike on the Prenestina, when a nine-year-old kid yells out *"A moré,*[76] give me a ride?" "Sure, kid, get on," I say. He's headed to the soup kitchen in Quarticciolo, to fill his pot with soup. "Where are you headed?" he asks me. *"Vado a spasso,"*[77] I say. And here is his surprised, ten-syllable answer: *"A spasso se va la domenica."*[78] And here are two five-syllable lines by Alfredo Fileni, at a dance at the Communist Party headquarters in the Giordiani neighborhood on the outskirts of Rome: *"Va avanti a forza / de vaffanculo."*[79] (He was giving me a piece of advice: I wasn't

---

[75] Slyness.

[76] Abbreviation of "moretto," which is a diminutive of "moro."

[77] "Just cruising."

[78] "Sundays are for cruising." In other words, don't you have anything better to do?

[79] "You only get things if you say fuck off!" In other words, you've got to fight to get ahead.

moving quickly enough to ask the girls to dance. In fact, as there were few girls in attendance, I wanted to give the other young men a chance.) And what about Begalone's hendeca-syllabic line,[80] as he relaxed on the bank of the Aniene River: "*Ciò na fame che me c . . . sotto.*"[81]

Orazio, Rome, IV, numbers 6–9, June–September, 1952.

The last part of the text, which includes the "verses by the most modern of speakers," corresponds to chapter X of the "*Appunti per un poema popolare*" ("Notes for a poem of the people," in *Alì of the Blue Eyes*). In that version, the final hendecasyllabic line, which is somewhat forced here, is more regular: "*Se dorme bene, eh?, a Largo Arenula!*" ("It's comfortable here, eh, sleeping at Largo Arenula!")

---

[80] A line of 11 syllables, which is the form used in most Italian epic poetry, for example in *The Divine Comedy*.
[81] "I'm so hungry I could s . . . myself."

ROGUISH ROME

I always tell everyone, when I have the chance, that Rome is the most beautiful city in the world. Of all the cities I know, it's the one where I'd rather live; in fact, I can't imagine living anywhere else. In my worst nightmares, I dream that I am forced to leave Rome and return to Northern Italy. Its beauty is a natural mystery. We can attribute it to the baroque, the atmosphere, the composition of the terrain, with its elevations and depressions, a landscape that continually offers new perspective, to the Tiber that plows through it, opening glorious airy spaces in its heart, and most of all to the stratification of styles which at every angle offers up a new, surprising cross section. The excessive beauty produced by this superposition of styles is a veritable shock to the system. But would Rome be the most beautiful city in the world if it were not, at the same time, the ugliest?

Naturally, beauty and ugliness go hand in hand. The latter renders the former touching and human. The former allows us to forget the latter.

There are few spots in the city that are *exclusively* beautiful or *exclusively* ugly. There is something archaeological about beauty when it is isolated, in the best of cases. Usually, it is the expression of a non-democratic history, in which the people exist only to add "color," as in a print by Pinelli.

On the other hand, ugliness, when it is isolated and approaches the level of hideousness, is never completely depressing or repulsive. It contains within it an allegory of hunger and pain, its history is our history, the history of Fascism, of the war, and of the post-war period. It is tragic, but immediate, and for this reason, full of life. In this city, hope is not political, because the sub-proletariat professes a strange, confused sort of communism. It is a pure hope: the hope of people who live before history, and so have all of history ahead of them. It is an anarchic, infantile condition. The crimes we read about every day in the paper speak of weakness and terror: people who kill in order not to be killed, who prevent evil with evil. "The early bird gets the worm," reflects a *ragazzo* who goes "downtown." He is always on the alert, picking fights, looking for trouble. His morality is the law of the jungle because he is in a position of weakness. The rules of behavior in a *piazzetta* in Trastevere, Testaccio, or Borgo Panico, and especially in any outlying neighborhood, are based on terror. High spirits, sneering, sarcasm, slyness, and cajolery are simply more or less inventive applications of an unwritten code, which, with some patience and statistical work, might even be set down, including the variations from one neighborhood to the next.

I would like to record the code of honor and behavior of the Jewish inhabitants of Piazza Giudía, for example, whose capacity for psychological penetration and knowledge of human types renders them the most plain, prosaic, and skeptical people in the world, and at the same time, the most understanding. They are capable of grasping your weaknesses and your strengths, and of respecting you for them. Unless you show yourself to be on their level, in which case they wrap themselves in a poetic, picaresque veil of mystery. And I would like to write the manual for the perfect scoundrel from Trastevere or Borgo Panico, surely the most rigid and conventional, within a certain margin of error, of course, because we are dealing with human beings. There is in fact an aristocracy of the masses. These codes, rich in traditions and consciousness, are completely reactionary, based on the narcissism and exhibitionism typical of Roman youth. It is a clinical fixation, and therefore remains unchanged in the older generations. For this reason, women are neglected and considered to be worth no more than a flimsy gold chain, a pair of stylish shoes, or some other ornament for the male person. As a result they are rendered less beautiful, and hardened. They take their revenge whenever they can, and are merciless depositories of the code, longing desperately for another code: that of the *petit bourgeois*, handed down from the upper classes, with whom they have frequent, if superficial, contact.

From the center of the city, the model of plebeian, sly, roguish life irradiates, and multiplies into myriad variations. It tends toward a less likeable kind of delinquency in the newer outlying areas built for the *petite bourgeoisie* that are slowly becoming part of central Rome. The same phenomena that are found in Testaccio in an advanced phase can be found, in a much more primitive version, in Garbatella, for example, or in Casal Bertone, which is a recently built outlying neighborhood, poor but not sordid, on the Via Prenestina. In differing modes and phases, an imitation of the principal code of conduct prevails: that of the lowlife of the Trastevere. But, like all imitators, the outsiders, the scoundrels from the suburbs, lack elegance, far outstripping their models in cruelty and carelessness.

In the furthest slums, the situation is aggravated. There is significant divide, cultural and architectural, isolating these areas in the slow development of the more squalid, disorderly periphery. These suburban areas are the result of Fascist demolitions; the first stratum of the population here comes from the center of Rome, from Borgo Pio for example. But on top of that one, three thousand other strata have been added: refugees, "urbanized peasants," people who moved here from Cassino at the end of the war, and more recently, people from the rest of Italy, but with a traditional prevalence of people from the south. In this belt of suburbs, from Tufello to Pietralata, from Tiburtino to Quarticciolo, from Quadraro to Tor Marancio, live hundreds of thousands of the disinherited masses, unskilled workers and unemployed.

Their situation is so rootless, so full of expectation, that what dominates their pagan morality—as modern southerners, or regressive Romans—is confusion. It is revealed in every act. In fact, I would go further: it is a neurosis. Not to speak of the shantytowns, lost under piles of mud, piled against the walls of ruins. There, we are beyond all definitions: there we find incurable cruelty and angelic goodness, often contained in the same soul.

Rotosei, Rome, April 12, 1957.

THE CORPSE'LL STINK ALL WEEK LONG!

I'm not a Roma fan, or a Lazio fan for that matter.[82] I root for Bologna. I'll let you imagine my mood as I write these lines. I think of the Bologna fans, my brothers in faith. It's a tragic story: I can see it here, in the faces of the Lazio fans. Roma fans are bullies, Lazio fans are heroes. One can't help feeling sympathy for the losers; the victors will just have to accept this reality.

The show is the same as it ever was. The best colors on show are those of the city itself: the blue of the October sky and the green of clumps of trees on ancient hillsides. When it comes to sport, there's no blue, white, red, or yellow,[83]

---

[82] Roma and Lazio are the two Rome soccer teams, and fierce rivals.
[83] Blue and white are the colors of the Lazio team. Red and yellow are the colors of the Roma team.

just gray, the gray of boredom, fear, and uncertainty. Bah. Same as always!

The youths who play every Sunday are bombarded with aggression of every type: rationalized aggression from the critics, passionate aggression from the crowd, and a bit of both (for good measure) from their coaches. And still, every Sunday, they descend on the field to demonstrate that the game is as it is, a concept.

A human, historic, earthly concept, and thus exposed to every risk and every negation and, naturally, to every sudden "creative" interlude (like the last fifteen minutes of today's game). It is the opposite of fandom, which is an abstraction, a fixed constellation, a dogma. I myself can't stand the, let's say, "Neapolitan" type of fan (and I know that all Italians are partly Neapolitans, even the *Bolognesi*). As Benedetto Croce would say, fandom is a "pseudo-concept." A source of error, aberration, and anxiety.

Have you ever really looked closely at a magazine ad? For example, a guy running at top speed, so that, at the very least, he should be out of breath. But only his legs are moving; his face is quite calm, illuminated by a radiant smile born of his faith in the quality of a certain brand of shoe polish. The "Neapolitan" fan is a bit like him. He knows, and is illumi nated (lucky man!) by a kind of grace. Reason is cast out, as is the reality and the experience of the actual match.

A portion of his brain (the main portion) is separate from the rest, and capable, while under the influence of that char- ismatic illumination, of only one fixed, immutable thought.

All that is fixed and predetermined causes immobility. It generates a mask, a caricature. This is humiliating to the man underneath. I feel pity when I see fans with their masks, billboards, etc. Nothing is more terrifying than the notion of bread and circus. . . .

Luckily, there aren't many of these fans in Rome. Practically the only "masks" around town are carried by the young kids you see with yellow-and-red or white-and-blue paper caps on their heads, their shirts untucked, their mischievous faces aflame, sometimes carrying the flag of the "beloved team." And the song they sing is completely childish: "We bottled them up, oh, oh, oh, oh. And they don't wanna stay!"[84]

The truth is that Rome is really a big city; the fan's love for his team is not a sublimation of closed, provincial, and municipal feelings. And the Roman *always* keeps that dose of skepticism and distance that preserves him from the ridiculous. What he celebrates in his team is not civic glory or athletic merit or other boring accomplishments of this type: he celebrates his own "*dritteria*."[85] And "a smartass is always a smartass." This description is apt for the working-class sports fan; but the middle class fan . . . well, that's a whole other story. In him, provincial spirit reappears. But, in this sense, the enthusiasm of new arrivals in the city is touching; their love for the Roma team brings a tear to the eye. They love the team desperately, and they tend not to shout; they

---

[84] "Li avemo imbottigliati, ooh, oh, ooh, oh. E nun ce vonno sta!"
[85] Cleverness, slyness, as in "sly as a fox" or "smartass."

swallow their pain and experience joy in silence. And they do not forget easily.

This is the opposite of the Romans, often young, who always have an apt comment to capture the moment, transcending it. What thrusts a Roman football fan into despair or renders him the happiest about the defeat or victory of his team is thinking about what he will say afterwards at the pub or at the barber shop. But of course, can a smartass ever really lose? And if he wins, can he really avoid making a sarcastic remark—magnanimous, of course—about the losers? My friend "Il Mozzone" called me from Torpignattara as soon as he saw this article pre-announced in the *Unità* newspaper, "*A Pà*,[86] don't even think of saying anything bad about the *Roma* team!" Then I saw him with his friends Patata[87] and Giancarlo, at the foot of Mussolini's obelisk. Their joy and ardor were evident. He said it all in a few words, as soon as we were within sight of Saint Peter's: "Write in your article," he said, "that the corpse was already starting to stink when we left the stadium. And it'll keep stinking all week long!"

L'Unità, Rome, October 28, 1957.

---

[86] *Pà* is an abbreviated form of Pasolini.
[87] A nickname that means "potato."

ROMAN SLANG

Slang is a technical language, and as such it is on the outer limit of usage. There is an endless list of books on the subject; one of the first scholars of Italian slang, L. Nicastro, was from Rome. Roman dialect is in most cases a form of slang. It is inconceivable for a Roman speaker, especially if he is young, to express a complete thought (which he would call a "*pezzo,*" as in "listen to this *pezzo*") without using "expressive emphases" and without making use of a "vivid" vocabulary.

What a Roman admires above all in a person are his skills as an orator, his linguistic inventiveness, or at least his vivid usage of slang expressions. "How about that?" says a boy, after having knocked off a particularly successful remark (a "*sparata,*" or "*sbrasata*"). For example, the film rendition of Shakespeare's *Julius Caesar* was a true Roman success, due mainly to Antonio's speech; I have seen young people from the most diverse neighborhoods of the city, from Porta Cavalleggeri to Primavalle to Testaccio, who can recite long passages from memory. Ultimately, Marlon Brando's speech is the speech of a *dritto*, a smartass. In it, rhetorical twists, reticence, and allusion predominate. It exemplifies the art of saying and not saying, of winking to the listener, with the aim of poking fun at certain people (in this case, the conspirators, who are noble of spirit, and thus fools) and mesmerizing others (the large crowd).

Slang is born in clearly demarcated groups, either of artisans or of thieves. But it spreads immediately via the conscious choice of speakers, and naturally through a series of variations, especially according to gender, but also according to age. If the language of men and women is different, so is that of the young and the old. One would imagine the latter to be more conservative, as is the case in the rest of the world, but in Rome this seems to be less true. Men are *ragazzi* their entire lives, with a touch of narcissism to keep the linguistic inventiveness alive—after all, it is a form of crooked exhibitionism.

Roman slang depends on this fundamental "narcissistic fixation" in the average speaker, and his consequent exhibitionism. Do we need proof of this? Recent southern additions simply underscore a traditional fact. And I don't think that a racial explanation can be invoked. The infantilism that causes the craving for a manner of speech that is attractive, amusing, ironic, treacherous, insolent, blissful, and almost incomprehensible—due to its underworld, clandestine references—is a historic reality. It is the linguistic manifestation of a sub-culture, typical of an underclass that is frequently in contact with the dominating class: servile and disrespectful, hypocritical and unbelieving, spoiled and merciless. It is the psychological condition of a lower class that for centuries has remained "irresponsible." Their only "vengeance" is the belief that they, not the powerful, are the depositories of a notion of life which is more ... "virile," because it is unscrupulous, vulgar, sly, and perhaps more obscene and devoid of moral niceties. This ruthless notion of life coincides with a morality which in its own way is epic. "*Vita*," or life, means "*malavita*," underworld, and something more besides. It is a philosophy of life, a praxis.

A *ragazzo* to whom I observed that it was not good manners to spit in a pizzeria, responded, shrugging his shoulders and looking at me, fair-haired as a baby Cain: "I live my life, I don't give a shit about anybody else's." [*Io fo' la vita mia: dell'altri nun me ne frega niente.*] Another time, when I was walking down a street in the Garbatella neighborhood, I saw a drunk old man spitting out guttural, blind phonemes to his friend as he peed on the sidewalk. I commented to a young man who was with me, that after so many years in Rome, I still couldn't get used to such revolting spectacles. He answered, "That's life." [*È de vita.*]

I don't know if there are any experts who are currently studying the lexicon of Roman slang. I, who am not an expert, rely on my tape recorder, picking up the expressions that I hear in the streets, emerging from the dark and returning to it. I heard a young Genovese hoodlum say *"mecca,"* meaning a woman, and have read *"zaraffa"* (pickpocket) and other underworld terms in Danilo Dolci's[88] reports from Palermo. I know nothing more about the etymology or origins of this lexicon. Here is a small sample of the slang of a small band of thieves, whose home base is a little piazza in the Trastevere neighborhood (which I will not name), told to me by a *ragazzo* (nicknamed Picchiola, Nicchiola, Negretto, Sciaboletta, Cappellone, Ciambellone, Lupetto, Zclletta, Sbaficchio, Luccicotto, Scintillone, Fumetto, Rabadicchio or some such). I will not even give his initials, as any self-respecting folklorist would do:

Pitonà = sleep
Farlocchi = pilgrims, tourists
Un tinello de latte zozzo[89] = a cappuccino
Ragagnòttolo = *ragazzo*, young man
Rombonze[90] = motorcycle
Svortà = to eat
Svortata = a big meal
Patatanza[91] = potato
Monetanza[92] = money

---

[88] Danilo Dolci was a determined and much-loved anti-Mafia activist from Sicily.
[89] Literally, cup of dirty water.
[90] From *"rombo,"* or rumble.
[91] From *"patata,"* or potato.
[92] From *"moneta,"* or coins.

Biranza[93] = beer
Lattanze[94] = milk
Mercettòla[95] = stolen goods
Viemme sotto[96] = give me the goods or the money
Cagà[97] = to confess, sing to the authorities
Dàmese, dàtte[98] = let's get out of here, get out of here.

This lexicon is deformed by its sense of pleasure and inventiveness; it is almost a form of evasion from the margins to the center, the inverse of bourgeois hermeneutics. But delinquency colored with bourgeois snobbery is the most dangerous thing of all. It amounts to exaltation added to hunger and anarchy. We see the roots of "pitonà"[99] (from "pitone," bringing back schoolroom memories), or of "rombonze" (from the upper class word, "rombo," or noise). We see the refined, somewhat forced parody of "latte zozzo," the extravagance of the endings -anze and -onze. And in this way, the rejected amuse themselves, the desperate find hope.

(1957)

Folder from the archive entitled, *Scartafaccio*[100] *1954–55.*

---

[93] From "*birra*," or beer.
[94] From "*latte*," or milk.
[95] From "*merce*," or goods.
[96] Literally, "come down."
[97] From "*cagare*," or shit.
[98] Literally, "to give."
[99] From "*pitone*," or python: to sleep like a python after it has devoured its prey.
[100] Notebook.

I'D NEVER SEEN ROME LIKE THIS

I walk up from Porta Pia, slowly and somewhat listlessly. The atmosphere is that of the edges of a public event: tempestuous, colorless, and almost noiseless. The first buses and cars stop, hysterical, here and there, complaining with anxious, brief honks of the horn. I watch the people who, like me, are walking toward the Corso d'Italia, or who remain near the Porta Pia. Some kids I can't quite make out have climbed onto the Monument to a Bersagliere, leaving a mass of scooters around the base. I see mainly older men, factory and office workers, and many women, of humble origins and not young.

There is a light fall breeze, and a northern, white, diffuse light. And a great silence, which the sounds, deadened and lacerated by the traffic, render even more strange. Already, on this and the opposite side of the Corso d'Italia, the crowds are dense: police officers stream down the middle of the road, passing by as if they didn't exist at all. There is no tension between them and the crowd. Everything seems suspended, frozen; even I feel as if I had been reduced to my eyes, devoid of a heart, pure expectation. But through the eyes, the heart is filled.

I have never seen people like these in Rome. I feel as if I were in a different city.

The Corso d'Italia is a curved street, under the walls; the crowd is boundless. A little old man looks around him, intimidated, and says to his friend, who walks next to him in silence: "Look. They've come spontaneously." Look at them, the humble crowd of his equals. I walk forward, along the sidewalk. As soon as I see a space in the crowd, I stop, under a tree; it has lost most of its leaves, but it is still full of the Roman summer that refuses to die. Two men (not boys) have climbed up the tree and are standing among the branches in silence, with their bicycles leaning against the trunk. A young, emboldened kid from the countryside walks by and looks up at them and asks in his heavy accent: "Comrade, will you give me a hand?" One of the two men in the tree slowly helps him up, in silence. In front of me there are four or five men in their forties and fifties, factory workers, some of them with their wives; the wives stand a little bit to the side, almost as if the funeral of Di Vittorio[101] were principally men's business.

---

[101] Giuseppe Di Vittorio (1892–1957), one of the most famous Italian and international labor organizers.

The funeral wreaths begin to go by in silence, a crowd passing through the crowd, both of them boundless.

There are thousands upon thousands of men and women, almost all of them dressed in clothes that are neither work clothes nor their Sunday best. They are wearing the clothes they put on in the evening, after they have washed off the grime and the soot, the clothes they wear to walk in the neighborhood, to saunter around the piazza. One sees neither rags nor the sweaters and short trousers popular in the suburbs of Rome. The people have strong, honest faces, burnished by hard labor and poverty. This is the first time I have seen Rome like this.

Streaming into the streets, surrounded by the silence that defines their existence, they are the greater part of the city, and demonstrate here the power of their consciences. They confirm that history never stops. The anarchic, skeptical, lazy, irresponsible Roman man has developed this expression, this hardness, this humble certainty. I can't say what part the man whose body today is being carried to the cemetery has played in this evolution. It must be significant, if all these men feel it with such spontaneous, disconcerting emotion. I know they needn't be told that they have lost a brother; they are filled with a mute, desperate gratitude.

The band goes by, and then more wreaths, dozens of them, carried by working men, working women, youths.

Here is the coffin. Fists are raised to salute Di Vittorio, in a silence loaded with an internalized, heartbreaking uproar. The men in front of me, one after another, raise their fists with difficulty, as if they had to carry an unbearable weight. They remain like that, with their fists raised, almost as if they were gripping, holding back something that they themselves cannot identify, a life of struggle and labor, their own lives and that of their comrade who is leaving them.

I look at those backs, slightly deformed by their labors, dressed in those almost festive clothes, the massive shoulders, the bony elbows. They are men who have been toughened by a hardscrabble childhood, work at a young age, the continuous difficulty of survival, the harshness of an existence that is reduced to the practical, and often even the animal, by the corruption of the neighborhoods they live in. They are callused everywhere. But when the coffin has passed, and their arms finally come down, I can tell from their attitudes that something has happened inside of them. One of the men in front of me cocks his head slightly to one side. I can see his long cheek, covered by his beard, and his red cheekbone. The skin contracts, as in a spasm. He is crying like a baby. I look at the others. They are all crying, with an expression of desperate pain on their faces. They do not try to hide or dry the tears that fill their eyes.

Vie Nuove, Rome, November 16, 1957.

THE CITY'S TRUE FACE

What is Rome? Where is the real Rome? Where does it begin and where does it end? Rome is surely the most beautiful city in Italy, if not the world. But it is also the most ugly, the most welcoming, the most dramatic, the richest, the most wretched. Films have helped make it known to those who do not live here. But one must be careful. The Neorealist vein that characterizes the films about Rome is too schematic, too dialectically partial, too filled with humanitarian optimism and darkness to reveal, with its medium gray or pinkish tones, the atmosphere of this dramatically contradictory city. The contradictions of Rome are difficult to transcend because they are contradictions of an existential order. Rather than traditional contradictions, between wealth and misery, happiness and horror, they are part of a magma, a chaos.

To the eyes of the foreigner and the visitor, Rome is the city contained within the old Renaissance walls. The rest is a vague, anonymous periphery, unworthy of interest.

Within the walls lies a beautiful Italian city which, rather than revealing uniquely classical, medieval, Communal, Renaissance, or baroque traditions, reveals all of these at once. If it were sectioned, one would see an extraordinary proliferation of layers: this is the source of the city's great beauty. Add to that the sun, the soft air, the joy of a life lived outdoors— never truly idyllic, bearing a dramatic core, and which therefore can never be boring. It is always alive, moving . . . Add also the fact that the *petite bourgeoisie* and *grande bourgeoisie* do not play an important role in the city center, which is still characterized by the lower classes, as in the southern and Bourbon cities, filled with fictitious vitality and servile paganism.

The Rome that is unknown to tourists, ignored by the right-minded, and nonexistent on maps, is immense.

The ignorant tourist and the upstanding citizen who covers his eyes can catch a glimmer of this disproportionate city, sunken into thousands of grandiose and disparate pools, if he bothers to look out the window of his train or bus. Before his unseeing eyes, clusters of hovels will fly by, expanses of shacks like Bedouin camps, collapsed ruins of mansions and sumptuous cinemas, ex-farmhouses compressed between high-rise buildings, dikes with high walls, narrow muddy alleyways, and sudden empty spaces, empty lots and small fields with a few heads of livestock. Beyond all of this, in the burned or muddy countryside, marked by little hills, ditches, old pits, plateaus, sewers, ruins, trash piles and dumps, lies the true face of the city. Here lies a deceptive line of homes that twists and turns along the contorted horizon. And now a colorful heap, grandiose as an apparition, on the unpredictable ridge of a hillside. Over here, we see an enormous gray wall that looms above the viaducts and the railway bridges like an overhanging rock.

It is not easy to impose some measure of order on this chaos. But certain types and zones can be made out, perhaps by gradations in the level of life. There is also a generic, so-called "residential" periphery, where the ugliness—despite the sun—is merely aesthetic. But the periphery of the underclass acquires a more dehumanizing, violent, inaccessible aspect, which is difficult to interpret.

The diagonals of the Consular Roads—the Appia, Prenestina, Tuscolana, Casilina, Aurelia, etc.—form another city around the real city, complicated by traditional agglomerations of people, by its inextricable but established "levels of culture." It is not clear whether this other city is centrifugal or centripetal, whether it forms something new or whether it amasses itself around the old city in order to assimilate itself in it, like the enormous campground of an invading army.

It seems to have been born by chance, to have grown to giant proportions for no reason, to live an existence which is neither its own nor marginal to something else. When one observes this phenomenon of the city that grows from year to year, month to month, day to day, the only way to com-

prehend it is through the eyes. The visual spectacle is so dis-
tressing, grandiose, and senseless, that it seems possible to
resolve it only through intuition, by a series of uninterrupted
observations, almost like cinematic "takes"; an infinite number of very particular close-ups, and an infinite number of
boundless panoramic shots.

The spectacle for the eye is inexhaustible from the Monte
Mario neighborhood to Monteverde, from San Paolo to the
Appio, from the Prenestino to Monte Sacro.[102] The building
boom has no limits.

Just as it is extremely difficult to describe the shape of the
city's advance (one would have to repeat oneself a thousand
times and find a thousand variations), so it is difficult to
define the people who live there.

Rome, as we know, is still teeming with the sub-proletariat
(Trastevere, Borgo Panico, Campo dei Fiori, etc., etc.), and
therefore with anarchy and crime. The first Roman factories
and mini-factories are beginning to line up along the Tiburtina.
The only robust industry, at least until a few years ago, is the
film industry, the "model industry" of Rome's working world.
It is an industry that does not necessarily imply a consciousness of social class, but tends to perpetuate a passive psychological state and conformism in the people who work there,
an attitude typical of a city with such a recent (and imported)
democratic tradition.

---

[102] These are all new neighborhoods for the poor built outside the city.

The hundreds of thousands of inhabitants of these new neighborhoods (and of the old ones, which were once almost rural, and are now completely surrounded and swallowed up by the new ones) belong, insofar as it is possible to define such a complex phenomenon, to a new Roman working class. In its dialect and vocabulary, attitudes, unscrupulous intelligence, moral laxness, and modernity, this new class appears to be the same as the old. But its more regular lifestyle, the cohabitation with immigrants[103] from the North and from the South, and its marginalization, a condition particularly vulnerable to bourgeois "ideological bombardment," have tended to mutate the deep mix of anarchy and common sense of these people into a kind of American-style indifference, a "standardized" type, repeated obsessively, hundreds of thousands of times.

Life in these boundless areas is reduced to elementary, monotonous formulas.

The problem of relegating groups of people to a system of marginalized residential areas and centralized work areas, and forcing them into an endless repetition of the actions that drive the very system of their lives will affect the future even more vividly than the confused present.

For those who attempt to look *beyond* the city's façade, the more immediate problem is an extremely simple one. Despite the building boom the difficulty of obtaining housing remains

---

[103] By immigrants, Pasolini usually means Italians from other regions who came to Rome seeking work, not foreigners.

unchanged. The 110,000 units built in the last year have not altered the situation. And then there is the looming tragedy of unemployment within the building industry.

From the inside, then, the city has two faces: that of those who build, and that of those who reside here.

The builders are few, and ever since the recent building scandal and the constant accusations in the press, we all know what this industry is all about. An enormous number of people live here, and, even if they are perhaps proud of their new mini-apartment on the seventh floor of one of the hundred buildings that crowd together here, they still sleep four or five to a room. The notion of well-being which the ideological influence of the ruling classes has depended on ever since the advent of television and pinball machines, and which is ushering in the Americanism I spoke of earlier, is in reality another form of chaos, misery, instability. It is even more damaging because it is fed to the public under the label of well-being, of betterment, while in reality we are still at square one.

Vie Nuove, Rome, May 24, 1958.

This and the two following pieces are part of an investigation that Pasolini did for *Vie Nuove*, entitled "Journey In and Around Rome."

THE CONCENTRATION CAMPS

In every Italian city, even in the north of the country, beyond the last kitchen garden, you will find the "concentration camps" for the poor, made up mostly of warehouses, sheds, and shacks. But this reality is nowhere as impressive, complex, and I would say even grandiose, as in Rome. The Roman *borgata*[104] is a thoroughly modern phenomenon that emerged out of the Fascist State, of which Rome was the capital. It is true that even today, these neighborhoods are being built. They are, in a manner of speaking, "free" neighborhoods, clusters of one- and-two-story roofless shacks, which have been left

---

[104] Literally, a suburb, or a peripheral neighborhood, but without the comfortable, middle-class connotations. People who live in the *"borgate"* are people who have either been forced out of the city center by real estate costs or very poor people who are moving into the city from the countryside.

unfinished for years and years, unplastered, lime-white-colored in the countryside and half abandoned, sparkling or mud-stained like Bedouin villages. The roads are mostly caked with mud or dust. Look at Rebibbia, for example: a certain man by the name of Graziosi sold the land in lots, forcing the buyers (builders who were planning to build their own houses) into agreements by which they also bought the road bed, with the promise that the city would soon build a road there. Some buyers agreed, others didn't (unbeknownst to the former), and so the fractioned road bed has remained just as it was. Instead of roads, the entire area is criss-crossed by dusty or flooded paths, depending on the season.

The Roman countryside, along the ring road, is teeming with *borgate* like this one.

These areas are home to people who are poor, but generally honest and hard working. Often they are immigrants, either from within the region or from nearby regions, people who have brought the serious and dignified atmosphere of the deep provinces to the chaos of the city and the smaller scale chaos of the neighborhoods they live in.

The real *borgate* are not these, however. The real *borgate* are characterized by their "official" nature. They were built by the city as part of a plan to cluster together the poor and the undesirables. This is their origin, both chronological and ideological.

The first *borgate* were built by the Fascists after having razed entire downtown neighborhoods. These urbanistic projects embodied not only an aesthetically idealized Dannunzian purpose, but were also, substantially, police opera-tions. Large agglomerations of the Roman sub-proletariat had historically been concentrated in the ancient neighborhoods of the city center; they were "deported" to the countryside, to isolated neighborhoods, which, not surprisingly, were built to look like barracks and prisons.

In that period, the "style" of the *borgata* was born. The basic inspiration is "classical" and imperial. Another typical characteristic is the obsessive repetition of a single architec-tural motif: the same house repeated five, ten, twenty times in a row. A cluster of houses is itself repeated five, ten, twenty times. The internal courtyards are identical: wan, dusty prison yards, with rows of cement bases for laundry lines, like gal-lows, common lavatories and wash-houses.

The city has gradually closed in around these neighbor-hoods. Before the war they were in the middle of the coun-tryside; now the city has swallowed them up, continues to swallow them up. Even so they persist, stylistically and psy-chologically, as "islands."

After the first groups of the disenfranchised were deported by the Fascists came the families who had been evicted from their homes, and then the evacuees. Then people began arriv-ing from Cassino in droves.

Naturally during the Fascist period, the war, and espe-cially during the post-war period, crime and delinquency flourished. The "Hunchback of Quarticciolo"[105] is by now leg-

---

[105] An anti-Fascist resistant and a popular hero who formed a group of bandits operating in the *borgate* of Rome. He was killed by the police in 1946.

endary. The thousands upon thousands of jobs created in the building sector and the introduction of immigrants somewhat improved the level of moral and civil life. Nevertheless, it continues to be among the lowest in the country.

We recently returned to the *borgata* of Gordiani. It is being torn down. Where there were lines of atrociously sad, dirty, inhuman shacks there is now an expanse of reddish crushed stone. And beyond it shimmers, weirdly, the front end of the Centocelle neighborhood.

A few clusters of surviving shacks are still standing, destined to disappear without delay. Soon the plateau of Gordiani will be completely leveled, and all memory of the neighborhood will disappear.

Most of the inhabitants of these houses have been moved, after a decade of battles and hopes, to the newly built Villa Gordiani and the Villa Lancellotti on the Via Prenestina, not far from the old *borgata*.

I went to see them. In reality nothing has changed. Instead of the small one-story shacks with a little courtyard in front, there are brand new buildings, amid excavation sites, abandoned fields, and dumping grounds. What are the stylistic, sociological, or human criteria of these new buildings? They are the same as before. This is still a concentration camp. Two or three years from now, these walls will be peeling, the courtyards will be filthy, there will be a shortage of space. In fact there already is. There has been no social renewal, no new social elements have been introduced, no liberation has taken place. The same people were transferred *en masse* from an old concentration camp to a new one.

The *borgate* built by the Christian Democrats[106] are identical to those built by the Fascists, because the relationship between the "poor" and the State remains unchanged. It is still an authoritarian, paternalistic, and profoundly inhuman relationship based on "religious" mystification.

To get an idea of what I am talking about, just go beyond Centocelle, at the end of the Via Prenestina, to the Quarticciolo, and try to maneuver your way across the chaos of streets in construction, the muddy fields and the building sites rising up in every direction, as of an Eastern city. Don't bother going in; you know what to expect. It's enough to peek in from the doorstep.

The first row of lots will appear before you like the front of a penitentiary. The buildings are about three or four stories high, in an indescribably sinister liquorice or antique pinkish color. You'll see an infinite line of windows and other ornaments, not without a certain air of grandiosity, in a typical twentieth-century Imperial style.

In front of the row of lots lies a road, teeming with misery and activity, down which rolls an ancient, rickety bus. An irrigation ditch runs down this road, its edges caked with mud and garbage, its waters murky.

---

[106] The Christian Democratic party governed Italy from the post-war period until the early nineties.

Beyond this ditch lie the newer lots, which were built in the last two or three years.

The architecture is the same as in the old *borgata*. The streets are laid down in a Roman grid, and along these streets are set the new buildings, all of them *identical*, in *identical* rows. But rather than being set parallel to the street, the buildings are diagonal, their corners lined up, so as to be better exposed to the sun—as if there were a shortage of sun in Rome. Rather than appearing classical and grandiose, the buildings seem Romantic and coy. And herein lies the single difference between the *borgata* of the Fascists and that of the Christian Democrats.

Vie Nuove, Rome, May 24, 1958.

THE SHANTYTOWNS OF ROME

You've seen them in *The Roof*, by De Sica and in Fellini's *Nights of Cabiria*, as well as in the various minor products of Neo-realism. There is no one in Italy who does not have at least a vague picture in his mind of the shantytowns around Rome.

But it's always the same: Italian culture in this last decade has been anything but realist, except in the specialized fields of the essay and investigative reporting, inspired by Marxist thought. This realism has only indirectly filtered into the artistic genres: movies, novels, and poetry.

In so doing, it has been mixed with other different, sometimes opposite cultural elements, thus undergoing an internal transformation. In the case of De Sica, it has been combined with a pre-Fascist humanitarian socialism. In Visconti, with a formalism which Gramsci would describe as "cosmopolitical," in Fellini, with a creational, or para-religious realism.

The fact remains that the shantytowns one sees in most more or less courageous Italian films are not the same as the *real* shantytowns.

In fact, I don't think that any writer or director would have the courage to fully represent this reality. He would find it too ugly, to inconceivable, and thus would be afraid of dealing with this "particular," or marginal, specific phenomenon. Certain low points of humanity seem impossible to treat in art; apparently certain psychological deviations resulting from abject social surroundings cannot be represented.

The bourgeois public would remain unconvinced by such a representation; critics would treat it with facile irony, perhaps attributing cruelty or psychological degeneration to the person who would treat such subjects openly and without hypocrisy.

We are talking about shantytowns after all, a form of habitation typical of prehistoric peoples. Ethnologists recognize the problem, the difficulty of conceiving an irrational state within a rational state in such a way that it does not seem gratuitous and schematic.

We are not dealing with the relationship between history and prehistory. Even so, the difference in cultural and social level between people who live in homes and those who live in shantytowns is determinant. Most of the psychological and social behaviors of those who live in shantytowns, in other words those who live with one foot in prehistory and one foot in the present, are irreducible.

Of course this argument does not apply to those who are forced to live there by external, temporary circumstances. These are the most painful cases, because it amounts to a true sentence. But for those who live in these shantytowns from birth, or by predestination (mostly people from the South, from desolate villages in Calabria, Lucania, Abruzzi), this argument is completely valid. These people are a true manifestation of the sub-proletariat, rendered more complex by the mixing together of the primitive state of life in poor regions with the semi-illegality and petty crime which is typical of Rome, as well as the general moral tone absorbed from the radio, newspapers, etc.

These slums are filled with illness, violence, crime, and prostitution. And these words can only abstractly suggest the human condition that exists there.

In Rome, there are dozens of these shantytowns. They crouch in fields and irrigation ditches in the cracks of the city; they extend along embankments and railway ditches, gripping the walls of the aqueducts for miles and miles.

One of these slums is called "Il Mandrione." At the end of the Via Casilina, just before the Quadraro neighborhood, there is an aqueduct; a road passes through the arches. To the left stands the ruin of a Baroque gate and a beautiful fountain. If you climb up, you enter a dark passage. To one side lies the huge wall of the aqueduct, and to the other, a rail line, lined with fetid ditches and piles of garbage.

There is a shantytown built along the wall. Gypsies live in the first section; then further down, under the second arch, embedded between two piles of ruins, there is a real village.

These are not human habitations lined up in the mud; they are animal dens, kennels. They are built out of a few rotten boards, peeling walls, scrap metal, and wax paper. In the place of a door, there is often a filthy curtain. Through the tiny windows, one can see the interiors, the two boards on which five or six people sleep, a chair, a few boxes. Mud seeps into the house. Even during the day, prostitutes stand in front of the doors to their hovels. A few motorcycles and cars of young men come, dragging in the mud. The mothers angrily call their daughters out to work.

A little door opens, a prostitute pours out the water from her chamber pot among the little children playing in the street, and a customer emerges. Old ladies call out like barking dogs. And then, all of a sudden, they begin to cackle as they see a cripple dragging himself out of his lair, carved into the wall of the aqueduct.

A group of adolescents watches the scene from a distance, with a thuggish, threatening air. Some of them play under the railway line, surrounded by filth and garbage. They are so focused on their card game that they do not notice anything around them, and play for hours and hours.

By the age of sixteen they often begin to work as pimps. I know one who, at sixteen, already had two women working for him. . . .

The repressive techniques employed by chief of police Marzano have eliminated some of the "color" from these areas, but it is clear to me that this is not the best way to solve these problems. And perhaps no one knows or is able to solve them through official methods and instruments. Even if you gave these prostitutes and exploiters and other poverty-stricken inhabitants an honest job and a home, it probably would not solve the problem. Their psychology has reached a pathological level. Perhaps, after all, a solution might be the rehabilitation of the psychology of these people through religion, but no one has tried it. Politically, these tens of thousands of unfortunate souls belong to the category of the proletariat. And on the other hand, how could one honestly tantalize these people with the notion of hope?

I remember one day, driving by the Mandrione shantytown with two friends from Bologna. They were horrified at the sight of a group of children, between the ages of two and four or five, playing in the mud in front of their hovels. They were dressed in rags, one of them wearing a little animal skin that he had found who knows where, like a savage. They ran to and fro, without even the sense of order imposed by a game. They moved around as if blind in those few square feet where they had been born and where they had always lived, knowing only the shack where they slept and the two feet of mud where they played. As they saw us drive by, a little boy, well built despite his tender age—he must have been two or three—put his little grubby hand to his mouth, and happily and affectionately, on his own initiative, blew us a kiss. . . .

The pure vitality which is at the core of these souls is the combination of evil in its purest form and good in its purest form, violence and goodness, depravity and innocence, despite everything. And for this reason something can, and must, be done for them.

Vie Nuove, Rome, May 24, 1958.

THE PERIPHERY OF MY MIND

I

The fact that when one is reading certain parts of *A Violent Life* one feels as if one is reading parts or pages from *The Ragazzi* is not accidental. It is evidence that the paradigm, the Spitzerian[107] period-in-question, is the same, and that stylistically, there is no major difference between the two books. If there is no stylistic transformation then there can be no internal, psychological or ideological transformation.

I conceived three novels, *The Ragazzi*, *A Violent Life*, and *Il Rio della Grana*[108] (this last is a provisional title, which may

---

[107] Reference to Leo Spitzer, a scholar of the *Divine Comedy*.
[108] *The River Grana*.

be changed to *The City of God*) in the same months and years; I developed and worked on them simultaneously. The only difference is that *The Ragazzi* is entirely, and physically, written. The other two are not; they are written inside of me and only partially on paper (*A Violent Life* is only two-thirds finished).While I was writing *The Ragazzi*, the structure of the other two novels was already completed, as were many particulars. *The Ragazzi* was supposed to be, shall we say, vulgarly, a kind of *"ouverture,"* suggesting a thousand motifs, creating a world which is "particular" but complete. The other two books were to deepen these motifs. In *The Ragazzi*, what counts is the world of the slums and of the Roman subproletariat as experienced by the young male characters; the protagonist, Il Riccetto, was a quite defined character, but also functions as a somewhat abstract thread through the book, something of a nonentity, like all characters who are a pretext for something else. On the other hand, what matters in *A Violent Life* and *Rio della Grana* are the two central characters, Tommasino Puzzilli in the first, and Pietro in the second. These two stories are in a certain sense "internalized," just as these boys' stories are internalized. They are abandoned to the streets, and their moral worlds appear prehistoric compared to ours, despite the intense ideological bombardment, the "bread and circus" they experience daily at the hands of the Christian-Democratic, Americanizing bourgeoisie.

The story of Tommasino Puzzilli is a kind of self-portrait: it deals with a character who is neither good-looking, nor strong, nor healthy. He is one of the weak, in other words, who must become one of the strong, in a world where it is necessary to be strong. He seeks continually to affirm himself, and we know where this path leads, to the pseudo-power of crime, cynicism, cleverness, or *dritteria*, as some people call it. Tommasino—who is not refined, but to the contrary, quite vulgar—reveals his tension superficially in his various political credos. He is a Fascist, an anarchist, a Christian Democrat, and finally a Communist. Naturally, internally, the story is more monotonous. The mechanisms, under the influence of external circumstances, are always the same. His friendship with some members of the Movimento Socialista Italiano leads him to become a Fascist; when his family is given public housing, after years of living in the slums, he becomes a right-minded Christian Democrat. And finally, tuberculosis and his friendships within the Forlanini neighborhood, where there is an active cell of the PCI,[109] lead him into the arms of the Communist Party. For good or ill, at the end, this drive to "affirm himself," to "exist," this aimless vital energy, is illuminated by a vague moral light.

II

I am so nauseated by the problem of dialect and language that the best I can do is to quote myself. Writing about Gadda,

---

[109] Partito Communista Italiano, or Italian Communist Party.

in *Vie Nuove* (January 18, 1958), I said that I found that this great writer used dialect in different and apparently contradictory ways, which I catalogued. The first, I wrote, "is a series of usages of dialect which imply a regression by the author into the context being described, assimilating its most intimate linguistic spirit, camouflaging himself constantly, to the point of turning this linguistic second nature into a primary nature, with consequent contamination."

This defining formula, while describing Gadda only in part, describes me entirely. Why have I made this camouflaging linguistic choice? It is in order, as Gianfranco Contini wrote, to make an "undaunted declaration of love." The sentimental, humanitarian source is part of my prehistory, but, as they say, "our story is history," and I would add also our "prehistory." I consider my realism to be an act of love, and my polemic against twentieth-century intimist and para-religious aestheticism implies a political position against the Fascist and Christian Democratic bourgeoisie, which is its historical and cultural source.

III

In *Città Aperta*, the piece was preceded by the following editor's note: "In this interview in which Pier Paolo discusses the novel he is currently writing, *A Violent Life*, we initiate a series of studies into the working method of writers, painters, directors, and musicians. This new column in *Città Aperta* intends to penetrate into the work and research methods and poetics of authors who are particularly significant to aspects of our culture. We asked Pier Paolo Pasolini three questions. The first referred to the links between *The Ragazzi* and his new work *A Violent Life*. The second referred to the relationship between language, dialect, and the characters in his works. And the third referred to his working methods.

I've already answered this question indirectly in my answers to the last two. I have no external method of working. The method is only stylistic, and therefore internal. There are certain facts which, in and of themselves, suggest a superficial, anecdotal notion of an "applied," "formulaic" method. In their satirical review, *Lina and the Cavaliere*, Franca Valeri and her collaborators have invented a kind of writer whose last name vaguely resembles mine. This writer (who is a woman, impersonated by Valeri), keeps two southern maids locked in a closet. When she works, she opens the closet and makes them speak. This is her way of "recording" speech, with a few corrections to suggest "contamination." Absolute naturalism corrected by a slight, but in its own way, absolutely "pure style." Apart from the comic aspect, Valeri is not altogether off base. If someone were to follow me in my daily life, he would often find me in a pizzeria in Torpignattara or the *borgata* of Alessandrina, Torre Maura, or Pietralata, writing down expressions, exclamations, and words taken directly from the mouths of "speakers" whom I have invited to speak for this very purpose. This occurs on specific occasions in my writing. For example, at a certain point in a story one of my characters steals a suitcase and a couple of bags; is there a word in dialect for suitcase and bag? Of course! A suitcase is a *"cricca,"*[110] and a bag is a *"campana."*[111] Stolen goods are known as *"morto"*[112] and *"riboncia,"* etc. (Instead of "etc." or "that sort of thing," in my book I will use "and all the holy saints," or "and all the saints," or, in less vivid cases, "and all that good stuff."[113]) I do not always transcribe this very particular, very modest material directly. I do so only in the cases when I encounter a difficulty or a stylistic need while writing at my table. When that happens, I leave a blank for the expression, and then go out to do research, which is usually quick and fruitful (I have a friend in the Maranella neighborhood, Sergio Citti, a painter, who has never failed me in even my most subtle requests). I also have a generic passion for words which leads me to write them down on the sly when I am struck by some sudden, unknown formulation. This then becomes reserve material, which I set aside, so that the next time I need a word I don't necessarily have to go to Maranella. At the back of the folders in my archive, there are pages and pages covered in idiomatic expressions, a small lexical treasure.

This is the only "colorful" aspect of my working methods. The rest takes place in the solitude of my room, which is now in a bourgeois neighborhood, behind the Janiculum hill.

---

[110] A *"cricca"* is literally a gang or a closed group.
[111] Literally, a bell.
[112] Corpse.
[113] *E santi benedetti, e tanti benedetti,* and *e tante belle cose.*

The difference between Valeri's character and me is that the relationship with these "speakers" is and has always been a necessary one. Every regression requires its a priori, voluntary aspects. It is clear that every writer who employs a "spoken" language, perhaps in its natural state as a dialect, must undergo this exploratory, mimetic regression, in the case of the setting as well as the characters, both sociological and psychological. From a Marxist point of view, this regression takes place not from one cultural level to another, but from one social class to another.

I feel absolved of any possible accusation of gratuitousness or cynicism or aestheticizing dilettantism for two reasons. The first is, shall we say, moral (it regards the relationship between me and the particular impoverished proletarian or sub-proletarian speakers). In the case of Rome, it was need (my own poverty, even if it was that of an unemployed member of the bourgeoisie) that drove me to the immediate human, vital experience of the world which I later described and continue to describe. I did not make a conscious choice, but rather it was a kind of compulsion of destiny. And because each person must write what he knows, I could only become the witness of the Roman *borgata*. Biographical need was combined with the particular tendency of my eros, which pushes me unconsciously (with the consciousness of my unconscious compulsion) to avoid encounters that could cause traumas of bourgeois sensibility (even the slightest, as experience has taught me), or traumas of bourgeois conformism. I am driven to seek the simplest, most normal possible friendships among the "pagans" (the outskirts of Rome are completely pagan; the youths there have barely even heard of the Madonna), who live on another cultural level. At this cultural level, the ideological bombardment has barely touched the question of sex. Therefore, even beyond the sociological need, I continue to live by necessity on the periphery.

The second reason is much more important, so much so that I could have even omitted the first, which I have succinctly exposed above.

It is clear that even a momentary, willful, experimental regression from one class and culture to another is also licit. I would say that this is true even if it were done for purely aesthetic reasons (if such a thing exists). Because no matter how disassociated it might be, there is always a documentary aspect to such experiments, an at least partially objective recovery of the world explored.

Before I began to work with the language of "speakers" from the outlying areas of Rome, and for similar biographical reasons, I did the same with another language without literary tradition, the Friulian dialect from Casarsa. And in a confession elsewhere I have described, looking back at a time when it was not yet clear to me, what the internal reasons for this linguistic choice were. The style I employed, despite appearances, was sublime rather than humble and obeyed the rules of the most rigorous linguistic selection, avoiding any naturalistic data. It belonged to the world of hermeticism, the poetics of the Word, and the invention of an absolute language for the purpose of Poetry. I am not sure whether it was as a result of the experience itself, or whether the experience came later; even so, mixed in with the stylistic furor of that Friulian dialect there was something real, objective, by which the rural world of Lower Friulia somehow emerged through the language. Considering the year (1947–48), I created with this method what could be considered the most "engaged" section of my book of Casarsian verses, *Il testament Coràn*, which is one of the fullest and perhaps best sections of my book of Casarsian poems.[114]

Today the two components of my inspiration—the sensual-stylistic and the, shall we say, naturalistic-documentary, political, component—are, I hope, more balanced. By descending to a world which has historically and culturally been poorer than my own—though irrationally speaking, this world is absolutely equal to ours, if not more advanced, in its pure vitalism—and by immersing myself in the dialectical and linguistic world of the *borgata*, I develop consciousness that justifies this process, as it would justify, for example, such an action on the part of a politician. Like me, the politician belongs to the bourgeois class, and distances himself from it, repudiating it momentarily, in order to understand and assimilate the needs of the proletarian, or at least of the working classes. The difference is that in the politician this consciously political act antedates and prepares for action; in me, the writer, it is only a linguistic mimesis, a testimonial, a denunciation, the internal structuring

---

[114] Book of poems by Pasolini in Friulian dialect.

of a narrative according to a Marxist ideology, an internal illumination. But this is not literature meant to accompany action, edification, projects for the future. Optimism and a priori hope are superficial things: I know that Liberty and Justice do not signify happiness and moral plenitude, and it would be disingenuous to promise moral plenitude as a corollary, or a mechanical result of the mutation of structures.

Città Aperta, Rome, II, n. 7–8, April–May, 1958, pp. 30–32. Republished as an appendix to the Einaudi edition of *The Ragazzi* (1979), with the title "My Working Method."

THE PROJECTS

At first, when I heard about the projects[115] I didn't know what people were referring to. I went to see them for myself when I heard about an event similar to one which I had described in *A Violent Life* back in 1957 or '58. When I arrived, I realized that in reality I already knew them well. I had never heard them referred to in this way because no one who lives in them refers to them in that absurd manner, but their existence had long ago entered my consciousness.

Apart from the fact that these housing developments constitute the setting of an episode in *A Violent Life*, in which the protagonist meets the girl who will become his girlfriend,

---

[115] After the war, the Italian government built public housing developments outside of Rome for the people who had been displaced in the war, or were living in shantytowns.

Irene, they are also the place I had imagined as the setting for a scene in the film *Death of a Friend*. I had derived the subject of this film from the reality of the Garbatella neighborhood, intending to re-elaborate it into a story, "Smells Like a Funeral."[116] As is the case when a writer imagines a situation or an episode, it was the result of a series of superimpositions. Seven or eight years ago I met a boy called Mimmo, who was barely an adolescent. I lost track of him, and then I met him again two years ago, shortly before he died of tuberculosis. He confessed to me that he had become a pimp, but he had lost none of the purity of adolescence: his degradation was evidently the fruit of desperation. This desperation did not mark his face or his movements. It was hidden and ensconced, as often happens in Romans. The evening when we met for the second time, he was with a friend, Lello, who was a bit drunk. He told me his story, which became the story of *Death of a Friend*, or rather of *Smells Like a Funeral*. He was an honest person, good-hearted, but weak and irresponsible. He could not find any real reason to resist temptation, and he let himself be pushed along, perhaps by a sense of the total uselessness of life. And in this manner, he too had become a pimp. Soon after, he ended up in jail for stealing a car.

All of this took place in the Garbatella. Now, they have built more of these projects on the Via Cristoforo Colombo, on the extreme margins of the Garbatella. But I imagined a

---

[116] *"Puzza di Funerale."*

meeting between the still blameless, though irresponsible and fatalistic, boy and his fallen, corrupting friend there. It was a superposition of images. It was there that I had met, or in fact only seen, another youth, Nino, who was reduced almost completely to his pure image. It was a sunny day, and everything shimmered, the garbage and weeds, tall buildings and shacks. He was standing in the sun in a purple shirt, his deep blue eyes filled with a strange, almost cruel innocence. He was a boy like so many others, with a job, or perhaps in search of a job. I saw him some time later, grown up and somewhat thickened, on the train to Ostia, with his father and mother, and probably some younger brothers and sisters. His gaze was somewhat cloudy, but it was still pure and innocent. He joyfully introduced me to his parents. His father was robust, still young, and seemed like an honest factory worker, and his mother, who also seemed young, showed the brusque tenderness typical of Roman mothers just slightly softened and mitigated by the fact that her son already had the bearing of a young man. A year or two later, I'm not sure, I crossed paths with a friend of Nino's called Bruno, and asked about the boy. Bruno thought for a moment, comically knitting his brow. Then he came to a decision and raised his hand in front of his face, with the fingers apart. He meant that Nino was in jail, at Regina Coeli.

This is a story that repeats itself thousands of times. And there is no reason for it not to repeat itself. In my case, or rather in the case of one of my stories, the setting is one of these projects, but there are hundreds of similar places in

Rome in which such a story could take place. These are groups of large buildings—not without horrifyingly "artistic" details like the stripes of marble that run parallel along the massive, coffee-colored walls—connected to each other and forming a continuous system, massed together like a smaller version of the City of Dis, modern and *petit bourgeois*.

Superficially, they are modern. But inside, behind those hideous marble stripes, life goes on in a manner that an Italian *petit bourgeois* not only would never aspire to, but cannot even imagine.

Under the mask of Piacentinian[117] solemnity lie the infamous rooms in which, as recent protest posters proclaim, eleven people sleep together. I don't think that the Italian bourgeois ideal includes sleeping eleven to a room. At the same time, the ideal certainly includes well-behaved boys and girls. These two ideals are in strong contradiction to each other. It is very difficult for a boy or girl who has grown up in conditions that imply, for example, sleeping eleven to a room, to believe in a kind of existence that would please the good bourgeois, the priest, or the Christian Democrat minister.

The surprising thing is that there are so many honest boys and serious girls in Rome. The old method of coercion is

---

[117] The architect and city planner Marcello Piacentini (1881–1960) was a leading protagonist of the Neo-classicist style favored by the Fascist regime. He created the Via della Conciliazione and other neighborhoods in Rome, razing entire neighborhoods in the process.

applied. They are given an insecure, poorly paid job, or they exist in a humiliating state of unemployment. Then they are handed a life filled with duress and unsatisfied desires. And they are given a home in which they sleep eleven to a room. In return, they are handed the notion of honesty and goodness. In other words, something essential is taken away from them, and in its place they are given nothing. They have only the duties of civil society, and none of its rights, and they must find within themselves the strength to appreciate and love these duties.

In short, morally speaking, the Italian ruling class is perversely tautological. In their view, the sense of duty and virtue exists in a vacuum, emerges by a natural force; it is not, in other words, the product of history or culture. And so they expect to find virtue even in places where there is no reason for it to exist. If the population of Rome, even the sub-proletariat, is fundamentally healthy and honest, it is thanks to its culture, which is still pre-Catholic; its root is stoicism and an epicurean spirit. It owes nothing to that celestial virtue which the ruling classes expect as a birthright, an obligatory fact.

Even from the paternalistic perspective of the Christian Democrats, it seems to me that the minimum that must be given to a group of people in order to expect virtue out of them, is a decent home. I would like to see how Scelba, Tambroni, Cardinal Ottaviani and others would behave if they had to sleep for years together in a single room. Mauriac used to say that men are not basically cruel, they simply lack imagination. What little imagination the leaders of this country have!

L'Unità, Rome, March 7, 1961.

On the evening of March 3, 1961, one hundred and fifty women (the number went up to almost seven hundred on the following days) from these projects in the Garbatella neighborhood and the shacks on Via Pico della Mirandola and Via S. Colombano, occupied three buildings of the Public Housing Authority on the Via Cristoforo Colombo; the occupation lasted four days, until the buildings were cleared by the police.

The episode in *A Violent Life* that Pasolini is referring to takes place at the beginning of the second part of the novel, in the chapter entitled "Stink of Freedom."

A DAY IN THE LIFE

At eleven thirty I must go and pick up Elsa Morante and Moravia; we are driving to the Castelli.[118]

Meanwhile, I have an hour to myself. I don't feel like working on my translation of *Antigone*, which is sitting on my desk, nor on anything else. So, instead, finally, I look after my own affairs.

I am in a period where everything has suddenly fallen into place, as if by some kind of plan; but surprises are always possible, and so are panic attacks. But I must say that all in all, the next two months, December and January, lie ahead of me without urgent deadlines; I can dedicate my time to marginal, pleasurable projects. I'll go for a drive in the South,

---

[118] The Castelli Romani is the hilly area around Rome.

and then maybe take a trip abroad, and meanwhile I'll fin-
ish *Antigone* and clean up the volume of poems *La religione
del mio tempo*,[119] which should come out this spring.

I am to begin filming *Accattone* the first days of February. With these projects ahead of me I can finally enjoy these
days without deadlines. Yesterday, for example, I didn't have
a single appointment. And I came home very late, after a
wonderful drive down the Via Aurelia, lost in an intensely
humid, refreshing, cool night—one of those nights when
sensuality dries on the skin, and the youths who are still out
and about at night in the towns lost in the darkness, show
no sentimentality and are cruel, compact, drained by their
own avid youth—and perhaps it is for this reason that this
morning I am so rested and lucid. I even have the strength
to call the person who, intermittently, looks after my finan-
cial affairs. I have been meaning to do this for months, but
never have the energy to do it, because I am so resigned to
the destiny of being swindled and mistreated.

And as a matter of fact, this call simply confirms this
notion.

P. C.[120]—the famous man who appears in all the newspapers—recently spent, as everyone knows, and rightly so,
untold millions of *lire* on a villa which he will offer as a
present to his stupendous physiological *monstrum*, she of the

---

[119] *"The Religion of My Time."*
[120] Probably Carlo Ponti, a film producer.

cartilaginous, kind soul. Well, he too owes me money, and the matter is already in the hands of a lawyer. It is but the distraction of a rich man who forgets what a million means to a writer. The matter has dragged on for two years. P. C. had asked me, through one of his people (he had just left for America) to co-write a screenplay with De Concini, based on Giovanni Piovene's *Letters of a Novice.*

I wasted an entire summer on the script. Summer, the only period when I truly live. When I say "live," I mean a matter of life or death. In this season, I thrust myself into life with an unreasonable fear of losing it. I threw away days and days full of joy and sunlight, purity, as I wasted away like a consumptive in De Concini's office, which, with its shiny furniture and closeness, became a representation of hell.

It seems mad to insert Professor S., President of the Instituto Nazionale di Dramma Antico, in the same list with N. S. and C. P., but. . . .

Professor S. is a scholar, a professor at the University of Urbino, a humanist. A large man with powerfully wrinkled skin like a rhinoceros, somewhat weakened by the softening of his hard edges due to good manners, and emptied out by his ancient Sicilian indolence, he appears to be a man of absolute integrity. But even he—not out of personal interest, of course—has, shall we say, "buggered" me. We had agreed on a figure for the translation of the *Oresteia*; the first half would be paid in three parts, upon handing in the three parts of the trilogy. The second part would be paid out after the opening performance in Syracuse.

But, to be blunt, I haven't seen a bloody dime of this second payment. And what is the excuse? Einaudi published—at the same time as the Instituto Nazionale di Dramma Antico—my translation in a volume edited by Gassman's Teatro Popolare Italiano. This publication competed with the first, and so the Institute, and specifically Professor S., refuses to pay me. I should mention, of course, that I had only given a vague permission to Einaudi's publication, through the director Luciano Lucignani, but did not sign any contract with Einaudi, and I did not receive a penny from them, and was not even given the opportunity to check the galleys (in fact, the Einaudi edition contains errors). Only I can know what this *Oresteia* has cost me in heartache, effort, even despair.

I also wrote a screenplay of *Girl in the Window* for Luciano Emmer two years ago. A clause in the contract with E. C.[121] stated that I would be paid a third right away, and would receive the other two thirds when the film was made. I am completely mad. And of course, I haven't seen the other two thirds of my fee, and E. C. pretends to know nothing about it.

Let us proceed, in order.

In the past few days, I've spoken with a lawyer about obtaining another "second payment." The person in question is also from Milan, the third in a row, a certain T., from a wealthy, famous family, like a Gadda character. Last winter, he came

---

[121] Probably Emanuele Cassuto, producer of *Girl in the Window.*

to me bewitched, I deduce, by two inspired directors whose
names I can't now recall, with a guilty look in his eye, along
with the two dreamers, an Istrian and a Sicilian, and asked
me to write a screenplay for him about Milanese teddy-boys.
I admit, I was truly a fool; this time, I really didn't see it coming. I intuited a deep honesty in T.; he seemed to me almost
like a young girl . . . the colorless hair, the moist, lost eyes. . . .

To make a long story short, I go to Milan, spend twenty
horrible days in a miserable little hotel working like a dog,
and continue working for another horrible twenty days in
Rome. I manage to pry the first payment out of them, but
has anyone seen the second payment? The beautiful thing
is that the two brilliant directors leaked photographic material from the film set to a gossip magazine showing some
young men, whom I had just met, actual teddy-boys, prior
offenders waiting for their sentence. One of them ended up
in prison for previous crimes, and from the captions one can
deduce that I am the one who set the two on the wrong path.
In fact, I had been around the two young men for no more
than four hours, to gather material for the screenplay.

Bitter, almost sick, I hang up on poor Onofri. And to think
that last night I was so happy that I began to sing as I drove
along in my car. . . .

*

Now I am speeding down the Via Appia with Elsa and
Alberto. He lives on the Via dell'Oca, and she lives on the

Via del Babuino; I pick them up in my car, and we're off. We thought—Moravia, as usual, a bit less—that we were unhappy and in bad moods, but in fact we are happy as children.

There is that humid air typical of Milan on rainy days, but which in Rome heats up and becomes a kind of double boiler that is good for the skin, moistening it, rendering it more elastic; the effect is not only felt on the external skin, but also inside, in the internal organs. It makes one hungry and awakens the desire for adventures.

It was raining, but it was the kind of rain that seems like a heavenly event by which water falls from the sky and the water, light as air, renders everything gray, splendidly flecked with silver, or white . . . there is a pool-like warmth, a taste of growth.

We are going on a pleasure drive down to the Castelli Romani. On the road we talked and talked. Finally, we could discuss freely, without arguing, more clearly and innocently than in all the literary reviews we had been asked to write in the recent months, with the joyfulness of helping each other to understand. And it was as if our respective experiences contained the same magic as the rain. We extracted from each thing everything that it had to offer, coloring it intensely—as the humidity colors things—and at the same time softening it, immersing everything in the relaxing rigor of tonal painting.

We cruise down the Appia, and we are already at Albano, where we will later return. We fly down toward Ariccia, clasped to its vertiginous bridge over the empty crater of a defunct volcano, later a defunct lake, and now a fertile funerary valley, gently opened to the sea. We reach Genzano, our feasting grounds. In Genzano there is a place where Gadda could not accuse me of lacking an "epicurean side"; here, I become a real gourmand and gourmet. Perhaps it is because the food is stylistically rigorous; the linguistically rigorous menu reads almost like poetry. Just as Elsa, Alberto, and I were saying a short while ago about the censoring of "good old swear words," as Belli calls them. Every text is a linguistic system, a selection, and for this reason certain words fit and others do not. Petrarch uses only a few hundred carefully chosen, "universal" worlds, and so even the word "leg" seems coarse. In Dante and Boccaccio, and also in Belli, any word is allowed and fits perfectly. In fact, it would be a stylistic error to banish any word. So, it is monstrous that it should be the censors who ban words. *Beccafico*, butterfly pasta with rabbit and thrush, boar sausage and prosciutto, roast venison and *beccafico*. Are these not perfect stylistic flourishes?

We eat with student-like hunger, and, for the first time since we've known each other, we don't mind when the guitarist plays and sings a couple of songs for us. Even Elsa, who is merciless on this point, gives in, smiling like a cat. He sings *"Spingola Francese"*[122] for her; for me and Alberto, he sings that song from *Maledetto Imbroglio*:[123]

---

[122] An old Neapolitan song. The title means "French pin," or safety pin.
[123] A 1959 Pietro Germi film with Claudia Cardinale.

"Amore, amore, amore, amore mio . . ."

Then we return to Albano and take the road to Anzio. The
houses along the road are old, of that wet cardboard color
typical of papal spots.[124] They are stuck to each other with
saltpeter and misery, but they are beautiful, with tufts of
green peeking out between the walls.

Just beyond, on the left, appears the valley below Ariccia
(there below is the bridge with its three rows of arches). It is
a strangely flat valley, and it looks as if it had been created
by a clock-maker, with thousands of tiny fields, orchards,
vineyards, ditches, straight lines of olive trees, golden-brown
thickets, sheds in the place of parts. The place we are looking for is at the end of the valley, before Cecchina. We can
make it out, under the messy clouds, like a line of white gold:
it is the line of the sea.

First, we visit the villa on our own, entering by the aristocratic lane, among metallic-colored vines, softened and
polished by the rain. Elsa must see it as she would if she
lived there, without the aid of demiurges. The little villa
stands silently under the light rain, empty and filled with
scornful, melancholy silence, gathering together a sweet
space of emptiness between its three sections. The central
section is in the style of a log cabin. The one on the right,

---

[124] The pope's summer residence at Castelgandolfo is on the shore of Lake
Albano, in the Castelli Romani area.

which has a garage, is in the style of a Canadian cottage, and the one on the left is humbly Southern in style.

Behind them lies the paradisiacal slope. At the bottom, behind a field that disappears in a brownish mist, shimmers the sea, yellow and bright.

On the right, peeking through dark, contorted fig trees, above the parallel gold of the lines of trees, one can catch a glimpse of the peasant house that I might acquire for myself. What a dream! It would be a kind of Chekhovian community in the Alban hills, pagan to their roots. A little house in all that golden countryside, contiguous neighbors . . . it's like a children's game! And peace, finally! Work in the eighteenth-century style, hermit-like, far from the city, in this golden bed of cotton-wool! All the work that can no longer be completed in this hellish, mean world. It is so pleasant to imagine ficti-tious lives. It is almost as if we ourselves become characters and our setting becomes an absolute setting, as in landscapes by the most moving Classical artists, or the calmest Romantics.

Then we go to meet the owner of the land and the houses, for the official visit.

Gildo Cicognani is from the Roman countryside, a noble-man with newfound wealth (he was in shipping, and now he is the president of a film distribution company, Euro). His age and physiognomy are difficult to define. He speaks with a nasal, grating voice. In him, the Roman accent is like a cold. As is often the case of nobles in agrarian societies, he closely resembles his peasants. He seems as clever as a peasant, but simultaneously vulnerable, and somehow worn down in some part of himself, by the decrepitude of a social condition which acquires energy only through refinement.

His wife is a Volkonsky: Yes, Tolstoy's family, the very same. She is a large-framed woman with an extremely delicate soul, fragile, which seems like it could crumble at any moment, or fade away completely, beginning with the too-feeble blue of her eyes.

They receive us in their country house, which was once a roadhouse and a tavern, now completely transformed, renovated to a feverish pitch, an excessive peacefulness, shiny floors, furniture all built out of extremely solid walnut or some other expensive wood, decorations light and serious as is fitting for people of a solid economic position and taste that is meant to last through the ages.

Then we pay an orderly visit to the property. First, the little villa that Moravia is thinking of buying, with a wide field in front, green to the absolute limit of greenness, and sprayed with rust, gold, and blood, then the smaller property which I am to buy, with a peasant house, still inhabited by a family from the Le Marche region, humble and warm-hearted, and finally, further away, beyond a daunting carpet of wet grass and contorted, temple-like fig trees, Elsa's parcel. She wants to live on her own, perhaps in a chalet.

It is a little adventure; the rain comes down more and more heavily, and amidst the green and the gold, one can see lovely, fatty, oozing mud. Stepping in that grass is like stepping in the basin of a fountain.

*

The scene: The smell of wet upholstery, double-breasted suits, freshly graduated students, women past their prime, men puffed up with *petit bourgeois* dignity, bearing the expressions of journalistic augurs . . . and, like two little mice gone wild, two young journalists, Adele Cambria and Berenice, looking for impressions. Berenice is merciless, Cambria (who will play "Nannina La Napoletana" in *Accatone*), is sweet and contemplative.

Everyone is there: Augusto Frassineti, who has become almost his own archetype, with drooping whiskers full of innocent, fearful, civic irony and Felice Chilanti, with equally desperate whiskers. Giacomo De Benedetti, "the great connoisseur of sins," palpitating and sharp, and Venturoli, looking like an explorer, a giant Renato Rascel, and Arnaldo Frateili, whose head looks like a snail out of its shell, blinking in the dusty light of the Ridotto Theatre.

Behind them stand rows and rows of friends, acquaintances, and strangers. I cannot see them all because they are already a crowd, timid and demanding. The two directors of the newspaper, Melloni and Coen, greet the guests, a look of quotidian exhaustion on their faces. Moravia enters, followed by me. He is fixated with the idea of leaving as quickly as possible, and so he arrives early, shakes hands quickly, and soon takes a seat, which, of course, is uncomfortable. I sit behind him, between Elsa de' Giorgio and G. B. Angioletti, immersed in the warmth of his large baroque-Lombard body.

Then Levi enters, late as usual, hovering over the seats like an angel with a frontal eye, like the figures at Knossos.

Frateili talks about the publication of the literary supplement "Libri-Paese Sera," mildly and colloquially delineating the sad state of the Italian publishing industry. Then Valentino Bompiani speaks. He speaks "well," as always. The panorama becomes even more alarming. About 30 million people in Italy are illiterate or semi-illiterate. But it appears that the middle class is starting to read, and for the past few years more and better editions have been published (the struggle has not been in vain).

Other publishers speak, and then, silence. Desperate appeals are made from the podium, which is vertiginously high up on the stage. Professor Russo asks for comments from Moravia . . . nothing. Levi . . . nothing. Ungaretti . . . (applause for the elderly, beloved poet) . . . nothing. Pasolini . . . nothing. The situation is somewhat harrowing, and, above all, unexpected. We had all come thinking that it was simply a cocktail party . . . I can't bear the embarrassment of the moment, and, it turns out, I do have something to say. I get up and walk to the microphone and quickly put together some comments. Then there is the quick, somewhat glacial, cocktail party and buffet; all the faces rotate around us, glasses in hand, bits of *hors-d'oeuvres* in their mouths. How I envy Moravia, who floats, untouched, here and there, in the fatuous waves of sugary, timid conversation, the exaggerated smiles of submissive admiration, the ostentatious cold glances . . . I talk to Pia D'Alessandria, and with Dallamano, who tells me of the terror he felt when I got up to speak. "Here we go," he confesses having thought to himself, "now he's going to say everything that's on his mind . . ." But Moravia tears me away: "Let's get out of here," he says, "I'm in a hurry. I have to go to the optician . . ." Patiently, I follow him out, forgetting to put down my glass.

First we go to his house to pick up the frames, which he is quite proud of. They are expensive, and they suit him. He is happy that I noticed that they partially obscure his diabolical, primordial eyebrows, softening his features. He is also happy that the optician, exhibiting a son-in-law-like sloth and rich sense of death typical of one of Belli's characters, recognizes him and exclaims: "I see our eyesight is getting worse!"

Once finished at the optician's, we go to Via Gaeta, to the Soviet Embassy.

I can't bear it anymore. Little by little an anxiety, which feels as if it were made of flesh, has attached itself in my rib cage and stomach. Everything looks dark, and I can understand why people punch through glass doors. A day completely devoted to social duties, even if it is within the more "lively" strata of the dead; I am suffering from symptoms of nervous anxiety, and a frightening darkness fills my world.

The Soviet Ambassador, with his vaporous wife, greets us at the end of a long red carpet, and next to him stands the new cultural attaché, in whose honor the embassy is holding this party. He is slightly plump and balding, and looks a little bit like Malenkov. His shyness renders him difficult to read; I hope he represents the new wave in Russian culture, which has recently revealed the desire to awaken from its fatal Stalinist torpor.

With his habitual haste, Moravia throws himself into the throng of diplomats and guests, amassed around a table as long as the hall.

As we look around us, we see only the cosmopolitan, homely faces of diplomatic wives and the soft, generous faces of men for whom irreproachability is a rule of life, and the bodies of women wrapped in clothes that are out of style and slightly gypsy-like.

Here is the face of an extremely amiable Russian, whose difficult last name I cannot remember. He is there with his rosy, sharp, eighteenth-century wife. They walk toward us, and, with extreme courtesy, welcome us. Immediately, we drink three vodkas in a row.

The correspondent of *Pravda* also approaches us. He is small and lively, a bit of a hooligan, with the look of a sailor on the Potemkin. Angioletti also comes over, with his wife and daughter. We propose a toast, on the initiative of the short Soviet journalist, to the ideological disagreement and personal friendship that ties Angioletti and myself together.

Then the journalist takes me aside and talks to me. I am very interested in what he has to say. Obviously his perspective cannot but interest me. He commends me sincerely, in the Russian style, for the few words I mumbled earlier at the Ridotto. I'm happy with what I said there, but it seemed quite obvious. I said that "Paese Sera" should not have a literary supplement like all the other culture pages, which have by now become the symbol of provincial taste and ideology and *petit bourgeois* sensibilities. At the same time, it should not to be too objective, in the sense of limiting itself to information that is generous and engaged. It should keep in mind that the lack of culture in Italy has a structural origin, and if on the one hand it is represented by the masses of illiterate and semi-literate people (thus limiting readership, as the *Espresso* once claimed, to the odd Belgian traveler), on the other hand it also produces indifferent, mystifying authors (when they are not explicitly slaves or accomplices of reactionary forces) who, out of a purely classist presumption, tend to forget their readers, closing themselves in their own, exquisite internal, "artistic" experiences, mistaking their literary products for a need for connivance and allusion. . . .

I accompany Moravia to the Via dell'Oca, and then I head home, exhausted. I have an absolute need to be alone. I dine quickly with my mother, and then I go out.

The night is a little bit like last night, except it is no longer raining. The clouds are like far-off walls, protecting the city, turning it into a kind of giant courtyard.

The humidity warms everything. What a magnificent thing these warm Roman winters are! And what immensity lies within this sense of protection! Our personal life is so limited that its never feels a sense of the infinite complexity of the other lives that surround it. It tends to simplify them, turn them into a backdrop. The humidity, the freshness of the air, tinted with warmth, encourage this laziness in the soul, this generosity which is merely poetic.

I drive around randomly for hours, in places that the authorities and Milanese moralists would prefer to believe do not exist. They do exist, and how! Between Porta San Sebastiano and the Via Cristoforo Colombo there is a growling mass of automobiles, motorcycles, and youths on foot. Every so often, a reddish police car, or the "hearse," goes by quietly, but no one pays the slightest attention.

Then I drive through Centocelle. I get out of the car and walk. How much poverty there is in Rome. In the summer it is less noticeable, with the sun, the blue jeans. . . .

As I walk, someone calls out to me. I turn around, in a bad mood, and see that four or five young men are walking toward me. I don't know them. They are shy, almost afraid. For the first time I see Roman youths in a state of complete confusion. They have recognized me—it seems incredible—and want an autograph. They pull out old, faded photographs from their wallets and ask me to sign them. Meanwhile, one of them, with dark Arab features and childish eyes, the bravest of the lot, says: "Now you're here, explain to my friend what you meant in your poem 'Pianto della Scavatrice'[125]. . . . We can't seem to agree about what it means."

I look at him, and then at his friend, a little blond kid who is trembling from shyness. They are both simple kids, sons of

---

[125] "Cry of the Bulldozer."

factory workers or small-time office workers. What can they have studied? They probably went to technical school. Part of me is angry: "What? I came out here to relax, to be left in peace, and now I have to start talking about poetry. . . ."

Perhaps they have perceived my bad mood from the look on my face, and this is why they are so unnaturally shy. But my anger is unjustified, and these kids are right. I gather my energies, which are quite limited at this point, and begin to talk to them, about myself and about them.

I return home very late: there is almost no one out between Porta San Sebastiano and the Via Cristoforo Colombo. Just two prostitutes, the tips of their cigarettes burning, standing near the "hearse," in the darkness under the massive walls.

The night, within the humid walls of clouds, protects us like a church. A desecrated, sacrilegious church full of sensual delights, vulgar and parched anxieties, and the pagan acts of the underworld, hidden, anonymous corruptions, ill-spent existences, poetic in their incurable misery, of egotistical hopes interrupted by nocturnal temptations, the humility of prostitution, the exhaustion of those who have spent the day working for a thousand *lire* and who, in the deep night, feel like they are reawakening.

The night, and life, are so precarious that a glimmer of moon behind the humid masses in the sky appears almost to be the dawn, and the dawn appears to be the glimmering of the next night's moon. I rush home, feeling a mixture of a macabre discomfort and immense joy, almost autonomous from my own momentarily ecstatic experience.

"*Amore, amore, amore, amore mio . . .*"

Paese Sera, Rome. December 2–3, 1961.

The typescript (entitled "November 18th 1960") is quite a bit longer than what appeared in the newspaper, and contains episodes that Pasolini later decided to eliminate. Once the cuts were made, the remaining sutures were visible. For example, on page 144, we find "it seems mad to insert prof. S between N. S. and C. P." N. S. was referred to in a previous passage, which was later cut.

THE OTHER FACE OF ROME

I would not be writing yet again on the subject of the slums and shantytowns of Rome if I did not feel that the problem today has changed radically, so much that it requires a new study in order to be understood.

The innocent reader should not fear that he is sitting before yet another paragraph of the "*cahiers de doléance*" on bitter human condition.

Chosen from thousands of possibilities, these images which you have before your eyes and that I am commenting as an "informal expert," are not images of Rome; they belong to Rome only in their secondary, non-essential characteristics.

Here we are on the outskirts of Mexico City, in the "courtyards" described in the stories recorded by Oscar Lewis.

Here we are in Partinico, outside Palermo, in the world witnessed by Danilo Dolci.[126]

Here we are in Calcutta, or outside of Lagos.

Here we are in Sakara outside of Cairo, or in the camps of Beja at Porto Sudan.

Here we are in the villages of Turkey, Greece, Morocco, in Cochin, in Madras, in the little towns around Tripoli, in Jordan.

Here we are in all of South America.

Here we are in Harlem and the black ghettos of the United States.

In one word, these are not images of Rome but of the entire Third World. Only in the Third World do houses emanate this gray color of rotten wood and corrugated iron. Only there are the streets as rough as ancient mud and dust, only there is the skin of children gray and animal-like, only there are the houses compact and den-like, and do the colors look like the background of a painting in the pre-industrial world.

Even though these things are here and evident, these images, in today's Italy, risk being *unseeable*. I can imagine eyes skimming over these images without looking at them, without realizing what they are. These are the eyes of those who "believe" that the slums are not their problem. They are so convinced of the extraneousness and untimeliness of this

---

[126] Danilo Dolci, a social activist and writer who died in 1997, whose passion for the rights of the poor led to death threats from the Mafia.

sub-proletarian, underdeveloped world that they would be unable to see it if it were in front of their eyes.

I am speaking of men of culture, journalists from the *Espresso* or the *Corriere della Sera*, writers, politicians, the elite of Italian culture, afraid, nouveau-riche and stupid, afraid to be considered out of fashion if they were to choose to write about problems that are seen as a thing of the past, superseded by a new situation of well-being and modernization. They are all for the "Seicento"[127] and pinball machines; they repeat the things they have read in sociological writings about other countries where people live in completely different conditions and have a completely different recent history.

The problem of slums and mud, of misery and dust, is not a particularly Italian problem. It is connected to the culture of Neo-Realism only because Neo-Realism discovered it for the first time. But Neo-Realism left things just as they were ... in other words, rendered them as a specifically Italian problem. But it is in fact a problem shared by more than half of humanity, people who are only now entering into history, bringing with them a terrible instability of life and ideas. Their war was fought in Russia in 1917, and then in Algeria, Cuba, Vietnam, and now, perhaps most of all in the heart of the United States, where the problem of the black population is not a specifically American problem, but brings together a situation that is typical of the entire modern world,

---

[127] A new model of Fiat that came out around the time this essay was written.

a situation whose historical importance is on a par with that of industrialization, technology, automation, and mass culture. The issues of hunger and technology are profoundly interconnected, and we cannot understand the former if we do not understand the latter, and *vice versa*. The world is composed of both and the contradictions between them.

In Selma or Montgomery, Alabama, and in Washington, people marched not only for themselves, but also for the people living in shacks in the Borghetto Prenestino, for the "immigrants" from the South, for the poverty in "developing nations." In these shantytowns the seed of revolution grows. Forget Neo-Realist humanitarianism and the aesthetic of rags! I heard Longo on television a few nights ago, his true, profound, and threatening words—threatening to the bourgeoisie, I mean—vibrated in his description of poverty, real poverty, historical poverty, the poverty of the world that is left behind, as it attempts to progress, with a violence that is sometimes conscious, sometimes purely a product of desperation.

Paese Sera, November 27, 1966.

AN INTERVIEW:
HOW BEAUTIFUL YOU WERE, ROME

Pier Paolo Pasolini's Rome, the Rome of his novels, his films, and his philological studies, is tragic and picaresque. He was born in Bologna, studied in Emilia Romagna, where he lived his hermetic period with Longhi, and then came his Friulian experience in Casarsa, his mother's hometown. First there were poems in dialect, then the first poems in Italian, and then there was September 8th[128] and the dangerous period that ensued.[129] Then came the end of the war and "my father's return from his imprisonment; he is ill, and poisoned

---

[128] On September 8, 1943, the Armistice was declared. Almost immediately, the Germans occupied Rome.

[129] Pasolini was called up by the Italian army in the days before the Armistice, and deserted before the advancing German Army.

by the defeat of Fascism, in his homeland, and by the defeat of the Italian language at home."[130] Then in the winter of 1949 he flees to Rome with his mother, "like in a novel." The Friulian period is over. "My notebooks remained in a drawer for a long time." "But soon, just a few months after arriving in Rome," he writes, "if on the one hand I continued in a baroque Gaddian note in my anti-Italian research, on the other hand I began to write that narrative thing which would one day be Ragazzi di Vita."

Almost 23 years have passed.

Yes, almost.

And why did you pick Rome?

It wasn't a conscious choice. What I mean is that, if I had had the choice, I probably, almost certainly would have chosen Rome, but I came here as the result of a series of family circumstances, because I had a certain chance of starting a life here, that's all.

You have lived here for 23 years. After all this time, do you feel that you are indebted to the city, or that it is more indebted to you?

---

[130] During this period, Pasolini writes and teaches in Friulian dialect.

Well . . . until about five or six years ago I had a wonderful relationship with the city. I wrote many poems . . .
all the poems in *Gramsci's Ashes* are set in Rome. There was
a real love there, if one can speak of love between a person
and a city. I owe a lot to Rome. I owe my maturity to Rome,
and I've said so in my writing, with the words one uses to
bear witness to a debt, in my poem *"Il Pianto della Scavatrice"* ["The Cry of the Bulldozer"], "Stupendous, miserable
city, you have taught me those things that, ferocious and
joyful, men learn as children, the little things in which the
grandeur of a life of peace is discovered, like going strongly
and readily into the fight . . . Stupendous and miserable city,
you have made me experience that unknown life. Until I
discovered that which, in each of us, is the world." But this
period ended five or six years ago. It ended not so much
because of a rupture in my relationship with Rome, but
because of a rupture in my relationship with all of Italian
society. If Rome has changed, extremely and for the worse,
it is not the city's fault. This thing was not born in the city,
but belongs to a degenerative phenomenon that is affect-
ing all of Italian society.

*Before this recent separation, five or six years ago, do you
feel that you understood the city, that you learned to know it
well?*

Yes, absolutely. But now it has changed and I don't want
to understand it any more.

So, now, you feel a kind of rejection . . .

Yes, I feel a total rejection and in fact I have bought a little place in the country and I'm planning to go and live there. And I travel often, far from Europe, to the East mostly.

So, let's speak for a moment of that Rome of five or six years ago, the Rome that you loved, let's say. If you were to anthropomorphize it, what gender would you ascribe to it?

I wouldn't ascribe a masculine or feminine gender to it. I would ascribe to it that special gender of *ragazzi*.

What age?

Adolescent.

What appearance?

The appearance of a typical Roman kid from the outlying neighborhoods, dark hair, olive skin, black eyes, robust build.

Robust, how?

Slim, not exactly athletic. A bit like an Arab, not exactly athletic, but, let's say, harmoniously built.

What kind of spirit?

The spirit that is born of a non-moralistic conception of the world. Not Christian. The spirit of someone who has his own, stoic-Epicurean morality which has, shall we say, survived the teachings of Catholicism. A morality which has continued to develop underground and to survive beneath the dominion of the Vatican. It is a philosophy based on a loyal relationship with one's fellow man, which substitutes love, understood in a real and authentic way, with honor. Tolerant, but not the kind of tolerance that comes with power, but the singular tolerance of the individual.

So, in your opinion, the centuries of Vatican domination have not significantly affected . . .

No, they have not significantly affected the Roman character. Rome is the least Catholic city in the world. Naturally I mean the Rome of five or six years ago, which was a great capital of the masses. Proletarian and sub-proletarian. Now, it has become a small, bourgeois, provincial city.

Why?

Because while the protagonist of Roman life was the people, Rome continued to be a metropolis, an untidy metropolis, messy, divided, fragmented, but still a great, confusing, sprawling metropolis. Since this acculturation took place, however, mostly through the mass media, the model of the Roman populace is no longer born of itself, out of its own culture, but is based on a model provided by the center. When that happened, Rome became one of many small Italian cities. *Petit bourgeois*, small-minded, Catholic, full of inauthenticity and neuroses.

Do you believe that this process of acculturation occurred earlier in other Italian cities, like Turin or Milan?

No, this process of acculturation, of the transformation of particular and marginal cultures into a centralized culture that homogenizes everything, occurred more or less simultaneously all over Italy. Several elements came together. The development of motorization, for example. When the diaphragm of distance is eliminated, certain societal models also disappear. Today the kid from the outlying areas can hop on his motor-scooter and go "downtown." People don't even say, as they used to, "I'm going into the city." The city has come to them. The adventure is over. The exchange between center and periphery is rapid and continuous. But Turin and Milan were industrial cities, not proletarian and sub-proletarian but *petit bourgeois*. So in those cities the change was less apparent, less dramatic than in Rome. This phenomenon is less apparent in Naples. Naples is really the only Italian city which is still the same as it has always been. With its own, particular culture.

When you came to Rome, first you went to live near the Portico di Ottavia. The fashion of fully refurnished two-bedroom apartments in Trastevere had not yet begun... And then you moved to the Tiburtino, then to Monteverde Vecchio, and now here, to the EUR neighborhood, in one of the most beautiful and quiet parts of the city. Is there a reason for all these changes?

Economic reasons, of course.

So, this pilgrimage upward from one neighborhood to another, and your personal experiences, have allowed you to traverse the various social strata of the city? And get to know them?

Well, no, I wouldn't say that. My Roman experience is principally the experience of the working classes. I have never lived among the Roman bourgeoisie.

You said earlier that you identify Rome with a certain kind of adolescent from the outlying neighborhoods, but don't you think that Rome is also the bourgeoisie, the small business-man, the restaurant owner?

Well, you see, this bourgeoisie is so closed in on itself, so lacking in a culture, so parasitical, that it doesn't even count in the city's life. At least not up to now. Perhaps the bureaucratic bourgeoisie and the government offices have counted to some extent. But still, this bourgeoisie is not very Roman. It has always counted politically, because it has formed the Right in the city.

According to you, Rome is an open city, in other words, instinctively democratic. Is there communication between the classes? Are there passageways from one social class to another?

No. There is a barrier between the center and the periphery. Until just a few years ago, they were two completely different cities. Now, on the surface, it is less so. But the reality is that the Roman bourgeoisie does not accept a proletarian among its ranks, even if he is gentrified. And the same goes for the aristocracy.

So the division is less evident, but more dramatic . . . do you agree?

Yes. It is more dramatic in that it is felt by the proletariat, who was not aware of it before. Before, the men and women from the slums did not feel an inferiority complex because they did not belong to the so-called privileged classes. They felt the injustice of poverty, but they were not envious of the rich, the well-off. They considered them almost inferior beings, incapable of adhering to their philosophy. But now the poor have this feeling of inferiority. If you observe the young people from the working class, you will see that they no longer try to impose themselves through who they are, but instead attempt to imitate the model of the student. They might wear glasses, even if they don't need them, in order to seem "superior."

And on the other hand, this habit that the aristocracy and the bureaucrats have of behaving like members of the proletariat, using dialect, going to simple osterie, etc. . . . this is all just a façade?

No, it is also a Roman tradition. I think that many of these habits have gone on for centuries. The Roman aristocracy, I believe, has always spoken Roman dialect. If for no other reason, out of ignorance. It is the most ignorant aristocracy in the world. So it is not even an aesthetic choice. Perhaps it has become so in these last years. But, in the past, I think it was simply out of boorishness. They had never read anything, written anything, brought anything to the culture; they were not even patrons of the arts, which is another way of understanding culture. They have always lived off their revenues, in total isolation. Mixing with the proletariat is now a snobbish exercise.

You have written in Friulian dialect and in Roman dialect. Beyond the level of experimentation, what is the reason for this, as a writer?

Well, despite the fact that people say the opposite, that they believe that my experiments in dialect have been instinctual, in the case of Roman dialect, this was not the case. . . .

What do you mean?

I mean that these experiments do not come from a direct inspiration. I did not decide to write in Roman dialect for the pleasure of it, or because of a personal interest in philology. It was not like that at all. My interest came out of an interest for this new life, these new people I encountered when I came to Rome. And, because this life and these people functioned in Roman dialect, it was natural for me to experiment in the language.

Let's isolate a few expressions which to me seem typically Roman. Why is an expression like "a fanatigo!"[131] so recurrent in dialect? Is this an unconscious choice?

Yes, it is a choice . . . What does this choice consist of? It consists of a Stoico-Epicurean Roman philosophy based on common sense, on a practical view of life which implies a humorous, tolerant condemnation of everything that seems idealistic, beyond reality. That's it.

---

[131] *Fanatigo* is a version of the word *fanatico,* or fanatic.

What about "faccio come me pare, si mme va"?[132]

Well, it fits into the pragmatism typical of all dialects, with a particularly Roman attitude. Like *"a fanatigo"*; there are variations of these expressions in every dialect.

Well, I don't know if there is another dialect with an insult equivalent to "li mortacci tua"!

No, no. These expressions are particular, but there are similarities.

For example?

Well, I can't give you a whole repertory right at this moment . . . but in the north, especially in the Veneto where people are more religious than in Rome, they blaspheme.

Can you think of any other expressions? Is there one that has left a mark on you, as a northerner?

Yes, there is one I love especially. It's *"anvedi!"*[133] It is the only case, the only moment in which a Roman lets himself

---

[132] From *"faccio come mi pare, se mi va"*; means "I'll do whatever I like, if I feel like it." In Roman dialect, the pronunciation becomes *"si mme va"* as it is spelled here.

[133] Means something like "imagine that!"

go. He reveals that he is capable of feeling surprise. Because his wise, detached, ironic attitude does not usually permit him to show surprise. Even if he is ingenuous, the Roman youth, or man, always tries to mask his ingenuousness. This expression, "*anvedi*," reveals a sudden capacity for surprise. And that's why I like it so much.

Il Messaggero, Rome, June 9, 1973. Interview with Pier Paolo Pasolini by Luigi Sommaruga.

TABLE OF DATES

1922 Pier Paolo Pasolini is born in Bologna on March 5. His mother, Susanna Colussi, is unhappily married. His father, Carlo Alberto Pasolini, a professional soldier, is passionate and authoritarian. Because of his career, the family often transfers from one northern Italian city to another. Casarsa, in Friuli, is the mother's home and it becomes the family's refuge during the summer months.

1925 Pasolini's brother, Guido Alberto, is born.

1936 Pasolini begins high school in Bologna; discovers the poetry of Rimbaud, which affects him deeply. Rimbaud represents rebellion, anti-conformism, and the power of poetry to Pasolini; Terence Stamp later holds a copy of the poems of Rimbaud in *Teorema* (*Theorem*).

1939 Studies Italian literature at the University of Bologna. Develops interest in Italian contemporary poetry, psychoanalysis, film, and classical music. Takes courses in art history with critic Roberto Longhi and writes a thesis on the pastoral poet Giovanni Pascoli. He will graduate much later, in November 1945, due to the war and his Friulian interlude.

1941 Hears a local boy speaking in Friulian dialect and realizes that Friuli's oral traditions have never been recorded in writing.

1942 Publishes his first book of poetry, *Poesie a Casarsa* (*Poetry to Casarsa*), in the Friulian dialect. The poems depict the bucolic landscapes and lives of its inhabitants. These aesthetic choices of style and subject matter will become a central characteristic of Pasolini's modus operandi. They are also brave moves, politically speaking, in a time of Fascist centralization of style and form. To avoid the constant air raids in Bologna, the family moves to Casarsa, where they will stay for six years. Begins work as a schoolteacher and organizes a Friulian cultural association. Involves himself in left-wing politics.

1943 Experiences his first sexual encounter with a young man. Called to serve in the army on September 1. On September 8, the armistice by which the Italians surrender to the Allies is announced. The German army mobilizes against the Italian army and populace. They capture Pasolini's unit. He manages to escape and returns to Casarsa.

1945 February, his brother, Guido, a partisan fighting against the German occupying army, is killed in an ambush. April, Mussolini is captured, tried and shot by partisans. May, the Germans surrender. When the author's father returns from the war, he is depressed by these events and feels like an outsider at home.

1946 Publishes his first narrative sketches, set in Friuli, in regional newspapers.

1947 Joins the Italian Communist Party (PCI), soon becoming a regional leader in the party.

1949 October, discovered alone with three youths outside a local fairground; accused of corruption of minors and obscene acts in a public place. Learning of the charges, the Communist Party expels him. Loses his teaching position.

1950 January 28, Pasolini and his mother leave Casarsa by train at 5 AM, bound for Rome. They rent a small room near the Jewish Ghetto. Susanna takes a job as a maid, and they live in extreme poverty. In a departure from Communist affiliations, Pasolini begins writing short pieces of fiction and reviews for Catholic and right-wing papers such as *Il Quotidiano*, *Il Popolo di Roma*, and *La Libertà d'Italia*, often under the pseudonym Paolo Amari. Discovers the lower-class neighborhoods in and around Rome. Reflects his experiences there in his writing. December, his trial for corruption of minors in Friuli begins. Found guilty; appeals his conviction.

236   TABLE OF DATES

1951 June, publishes "Il Ferrobedò," the story that will later
become the first chapter of *The Ragazzi*, in the magazine *Paragone*. Later in the summer, meets the eighteen-
year-old Sergio Citti, a young Roman hustler fresh out
of jail, who will become his guide to Roman slums and
slang. Meets modernist poet Giuseppe Ungaretti and
experimental novelist Carlo Emilio Gadda. Teaches in
a private middle school from 1951 to 1953. Now that
Pasolini is able to afford better housing, his mother no
longer has to work as a maid. The father joins them and
is barely tolerated.

1952 April, cleared of charges in the corruption of minors
case.

1953 Obtains contract to write *The Ragazzi*. Quits teaching.

1954 Collaborates with the poet, essayist, and novelist Giorgio
Bassani on his first screenplay, *La donna del fiume*
(*Woman of the River*). Pasolini contributes mainly by in-
troducing lowlife characters into the story. Publishes a
collection of his Friulian poems, *La meglio gioventù* (*The
Best of Youth*, as yet not translated into English). The
family moves to the more middle-class neighborhood of
Monteverde Nuovo, behind Vatican City.

1955 May, publishes *Ragazzi di vita* (*The Ragazzi*); the first
edition sells out by June. The government condemns

the book for its pornographic content, its rough slang, and depiction of sensual behavior by members of the lower classes. The Left attacks the book for its amoral stance and rarefied use of dialect. Along with some friends from the University of Bologna, Pasolini puts together the literary journal, *Officina* (*Workshop*), which will publish polemical cultural criticism.

1956 Tried with his publisher, Aldo Garzanti, for obscenity in relation to the publication of *The Ragazzi*. Both are absolved. In *Officina*, attacks the Soviet Communist Party for its invasion of Hungary; the Italian Communist Party launches criticism against him as a direct result.

1957–1961 Collaborates on numerous screenplays, including *Il Bell'Antonio* (*Handsome Antonio*, though the film was released in America under its original title) and *Le Notti di Cabiria* (*Nights of Cabiria*).

1957 Publishes the collection of poems *Le ceneri di Gramsci* (*Gramsci's Ashes*), a reflection on his personal history and political disillusionment. Achieves general critical acclaim with this collection, and is awarded the prestigious Premio Viareggio.

1958 Carlo Alberto Pasolini dies on December 19.

1959 May, publishes *Una vita violenta* (*A Violent Life*), a novel
set in the same world as *The Ragazzi,* and receives wide
praise. However, the Catholic Church attacks the book
for obscenity and the Communist Party bemoans its in-
sufficient solidarity. Summer, translates the *Oresteia.*
July, press reports accuse him of attempted corruption
of minors. The case never goes to court.

1960 Summer, writes the screenplay of his first film, *Accatone,* with the help of Sergio Citti. October, publishes
Passione e ideologia (*Passion and Ideology*), a collection
of literary criticism. The company of the star film and
stage actor, Vittorio Gassman, performs his *Oresteia.*

1961 April, selects a cast of amateur actors from the neighborhoods depicted in *Accatone*; begins shooting.
August 31, presents the film at the Venice Film Festival. It draws criticism for its depiction of prostitution,
which is considered overly crude and sympathetic. May,
publishes *La religione del mio tempo* (*The Religion of
My Time*), a collection of polemic, anti-capitalist poems.
Writes the screenplay for *Mamma Roma* with Sergio
Citti's help. November, accused by a young gas station
attendant of armed robbery.

1962 In the trial over the alleged armed robbery, a psy-
chologist describes Pasolini as "a psychopath ... a
sexual anomaly, a homophile in the most complete

sense of the word." Films *Mamma Roma*, with Anna Magnani, which is shown at the Venice Film Festival. The public prosecutor accuses the film of obscenity for its use of crude language; the case is thrown out in September.

1963 Meets Ninetto Davoli, a fourteen-year-old from the outskirts of Rome, while filming the short, *La Ricotta* (*Ricotta*). Davoli will appear in several of Pasolini's works as he embodies the figure of the innocent, "pagan," urban youth. Davoli later becomes Pasolini's companion, although eventually he will leave Pasolini and get married. March, *La Ricotta* is released as part of the omnibus film *RoGoPaG*, directed by Roberto Rossellini, Ugo Gregoretti, Jean-Luc Godard, and Pier Paolo Pasolini. The authorities immediately seize it and charge it as an attack on the state. Pasolini then films two documentaries, one of them about Russia, *La Rabbia* (*Rage*), and the other about sexuality and homosexuality, *Comizi d'amore* (*Love Meetings*).

1964 The charges against *RoGoPaG* are dropped. After collaborating for months with the Franciscan friars of Assisi in researching the life of St. Matthew, begins filming *The Gospel According to St. Matthew*. Releases the film in September at the Venice Film Festival, where it wins the special jury prize. The Catholic Church praises the film.

1965 Films *Hawks and Sparrows,* an allegory about the crisis of Marxism. It stars Davoli, Totò, the famous Neapolitan comedian, and a trained crow. September, travels to New York and meets the poet Allen Ginsberg. This visit inspires the film *Teorema (Theorem).* Publishes the collection of stories *Alì dagli occhi (Ali of the Blue Eyes).*

1966 March, suffers from a bleeding ulcer and spends a month in convalescence. Writes six tragedies: *Calderòn, Pilade, Affabulazione, Porcile, Orgia,* and *Bestia da stile (Calderón, Pylades, Confabulation, Pigsty, Orgy,* and *Stylish Beast).*

1967 April, travels to Morocco to film *Oedipus Rex,* starring the actress Silvana Mangano, along with himself as High Priest. The film is openly autobiographical.

1968 Cleared of wrongdoing in the 1962 case of armed robbery, bringing an end to the longstanding scandal that has focused on Pasolini's homosexuality. March, *Teorema (Theorem)* is released. A novel with the same title also appears in March. The English actor Terence Stamp appears nude in this symbolic story of the seduction of a bourgeois family by an erotic Christ figure. The authorities temporarily sequester the film for obscenity in September. During worldwide student riots, Pasolini attacks the "bourgeois" protesters and defends the "proletarian" police forces in the polemical collection of poems *Il Pci ai giovani!* (*The Commu-nist Party to the Young!*). The Left criticizes him for the work.

1969   Releases *Porcile,* an allegory in which the marginalized figures of a cannibal and a coprophile are devoured by animals representing fascism and conformism. Films *Medea,* with Maria Callas in the title role.

1970   Releases *Medea.* Directs *The Decameron,* set in the streets of Naples rather than in Boccaccio's Tuscany. The film is the first part of a trilogy that will include *The Canterbury Tales* (1971), and *Arabian Nights* (1974).

1971   Receives an award at the Berlin Film Festival for *The Decameron,* which is hugely successful in Italy and abroad. The film is also repeatedly attacked for ob-scenity. Publishes the collection of poetry *Trasumanar e organizzar* (*Transcend and Organize*). Becomes editor-in-chief of *Lotta Continua,* a left-wing news-paper. Perpetuates his ambiguous stance toward the Left with the explanation that "I can no longer believe in Revolution, but I cannot but be on the side of the young people who are fighting for it.... I no longer believe in dialectics and contradictions, only in pure opposition." The court in Turin accuses Pasolini of "polemical content regarding the armed forces," but the trial never takes place.

1972 Travels to England to shoot *The Canterbury Tales*. The film wins an award at the Berlin festival. The Italian authorities confiscate it for obscenity. April, publishes his volume of essays *Empirismo eretico* (*Heretical Empiricism*). Complains in these pieces of feeling isolated and obsolete. Lives in the countryside near Rome. Begins to write the novel *Petrolio*, a visionary, sprawling allegorical reflection on his sexuality. Only a fragment of the novel will be published much later, in 1992.

1973 Begins to write political articles in the *Corriere della Sera*, a respected, Right-leaning newspaper. Attacks the political youth movements of both the Left and the Right. Travels to Yemen, Eritrea, Afghanistan, and Nepal to shoot *Arabian Nights*.

1974 The Special Jury Prize at Cannes awards Pasolini for *Arabian Nights*. June, referendum legalizes divorce in Italy. In *Corriere della Sera*, Pasolini criticizes divorce as a sign of hedonistic, consumeristic, neo-Capitalist, American values. Begins work on *Salò, or The 120 Days of Sodom*, an allegory of Fascism and consumerism as sadomasochistic torture. The film will only be released posthumously in 1975.

1975 January, writes an article against abortion. May, publishes the collection of Friulian-dialect poems *La nuova gioventù* (*The New Youth*), a nihilistic revision of his youthful Friulian poems. Summer, calls for Nuremberg-style trials for the leaders of the right-wing Christian Democrat party. October, turns in his manuscript of *La divina mimesis* (*Divine Mimesis*), a commentary in verse on the *Divine Comedy*. November 1, gives an interview on camera to Furio Colombo. Later that day, dines with Ninetto Davoli and his family. That night, his body is found near the road leading from Rome to the beach at Ostia. Later, a young hustler named Pino Pelosi is found guilty of the murder. The circumstances are never fully explained.

Sources:

Bazzocchi, M. A. (1998). *Pier Paolo Pasolini*. Milano: Mondadori.
Naldini, N. (1989). *Vita di Pasolini*. Torino: Einaudi.

FILMOGRAPHY OF WORKS
DIRECTED BY PIER PAOLO PASOLINI

Accatone (1961)*

Mamma Roma (1962)

"*La Ricotta*" segment in *Laviamoci il cervello / Let's Have a Brainwash* (1962)*

La Rabbia / Rage (1963)

Il Vangelo secondo Matteo / The Gospel According to St. Matthew (1964)*

Le Mura di Sana / The Walls of Sana (1964)

Comizi d'amore / Love Meetings (1964)*

Il Padre Selvaggio / The Savage Father (1965)

Uccellacci e Uccellini / Hawks and Sparrows (1966)*

"*La Terra vista dalla Luna*" / "*The Earth Seen from the Moon*" segment in *Le Streghe / The Witches* (1966)*

Edipo Re / Oedipus Rex (1967)*

Teorema / Theorem (1968)*

"*Che cosa sono le nuvole?*" / "*What Are Clouds?*" segment in *Capriccio all'italiana / Caprice Italian Style* (1968)*

"*La Sequenza del fiore di carta*" / "*The Sequence of the Paper Flower*" segment in *Amore e rabbia / Love and Anger* (1969)*

Porcile / Pigpen (1969)*

Medea (1969)

Appunti per un film sull'India / Notes for a Film about India (1969)

Appunti per una Orestiade africana / Notes for an African Orestes (1970)*

Il Decameron / The Decameron (1970)*

Appunti per un romanzo dell'immondezza / Notes for a Novel of Trash (1970)

Racconti di Canterbury / The Canterbury Tales (1971)*

Dodici dicembre 1972 / December 12th, 1972 (uncredited) (1972)

Il Fiore delle mille e una notte / Arabian Nights (1974)*

Salò o le 120 giornate di Sodoma / Salo, or The 120 Days of Sodom (1975)*

---

* Released in an English language version.

BIBLIOGRAPHY OF WORKS
BY PIER PAOLO PASOLINI

Poesie a Casarsa / *Poems to Casarsa* (1942)

Poesie / *Poems* (1945)

I pianti / *The Cries* (1946)

La meglio gioventù / *The Best Youth* (1954)

Il canto popolare / *Songs of the People* (1954)

Ragazzi di vita (1955; *The Ragazzi*, 1968)*

Le ceneri di Gramsci / *Gramsci's Ashes* (1957)

L'usignolo della Chiesa Cattolica / *Nightingale of the Catholic Church* (1958)

Una vita violenta (1959; *A Violent Life*, 1968)*

Translation of The Oresteia (1960)

Donne di Roma / *Women of Rome* (1960)

Passione e ideologia / *Passion and Ideology* (1960)

Roma 1950, diario / *Rome 1950, a Diary* (1960)

Sonetto primaverile / *Spring Sonnet* (1960)

La religione del mio tempo / *The Religion of My Time* (1961)

Mamma Roma / *Mother Rome* (1962)

Il sogno di una cosa / *Dreaming of One Thing* (1962)

Il vantone di Plauto / *Translation of "Miles Gloriosus" by Plautos* (1963)

Poesia in forma di rosa / *Poetry in the Shape of a Rose* (1964)

Alì dagli occhi azzurri / *Ali of the Blue Eyes* (1965)

Orgia / Orgy (1969)

Trasumanar e organizzar / Transcend and Organize (1971)

Empirismo eretico (1972; *Heretical Empiricism,* 1988)*

Calderòn (1973)

Il padre selvaggio / The Savage Father (1975)

Scritti corsari / Pirate Writings (1975)

La divina mimesis / Divine Mimesis (1975)

La nuova giuventù / The New Youth (1975)

Trilogia della vita / Trilogy of Life (1975)

Le poesie / Poetry (1975)

Lettere agli amici / Letters to Friends (1976)

Lettere luterane / Lutheran Letters (1977)

Affabulazione, Pilade / Affabulation, Pylades (1977)

Le belle bandiere / Beautiful Flags (1977)

San Paolo / Saint Paul (1977)

Cinema in forma di poesia / Cinema in the Shape of Poetry (1979)

Amado mio / My Love (1982)

Atti impuri / Impure Acts (1982)

Lettere 1940–1954 / Letters 1940–1954 (1986)

Lettere 1955–1975 / Letters 1955–1975 (1988)

Petrolio (1992; *Petrolio,* 1997)*

Un paese di temporali e di primule / A Land of Tempests and Primroses (1993)

---

* Translated into English.

Printed in the United States
by Baker & Taylor Publisher Services